TEN PAST TWO

SUELITA CONSTANCE

Copyright © 2022 by Suelita Constance

All rights reserved.

No part of this book may be reproduced, distributed, or transmitted in any form or by any electronic or mechanical means, including information storage and retrieval systems, without written permission from the author, except for the use of brief quotations in a book review.

This book is a work of fiction. Names, characters, places and incidents either are the product of the author's imagination or are used fictitiously, and any resemblance to actual persons, living or dead, business establishments, events or locals is entirely coincidental.

Editing by Britt Tayler

Front cover by Daria Ustinova

Back cover by Daniela Silva

My dad always used to say: Focus on the ball, focus on your tactic, focus on your match, not how others play on the court next to yours.

I think I finally understand it.

PROLOGUE

Afterward, her memories from the race were vague. Other sources had tried to tell her what happened, but everything was a big blur.

She would rather not think about the things she so badly wanted, but could no longer have. She would rather not replay the scene of her smashed-up car and the blood running down her skin in her mind. She would rather not think of what her life was going to look like now, racing excluded.

It was a bright morning in the beginning of May. Nothing special had happened yet, and everything was great—at least for Lotte.

It was early; only a few sunbeams had been able to fight their way through the curtains, casting her room in a soft glow. She was used to getting out of bed early in the mornings, despite being up late dancing until her legs felt numb, drowning in neon lights, the night before. This day was no exception, and her nerves wouldn't let her sleep anyway.

She sat up on the edge of her king-size bed and looked down

at her feet, trying to make her brain realize it was time to start functioning. As she stood up, she placed her long brown hair over her shoulders and blinked her hazel eyes a few times while looking at her exhausted yet excited face through the mirror in her room. This day was a big day; she was going to give it her all, no matter what it took—at least that's what she thought at that very moment.

She started her morning by walking downstairs to the kitchen. On her way down the hallway, in one of her slightly too-grand houses, she wandered past large framed posters and photos of herself, along with the trophies bearing her name she'd dreamed of collecting since she was a little girl. But she didn't bother giving them a single glance, like others may have done, walking past such an impressive collection. She was confident that she'd see them many more times and that many new, even greater trophies, would be added in the coming years. As such, Lotte hurried along down the stairs, dancing her way to the kitchen.

She grabbed one of her fancy, overpriced crystal wine glasses and sipped on some chocolate milk she found in her fridge until the whole glass was empty. *Only the best for one of the best racers in the world,* she heard herself think, with a bit of an eye-roll. She was truly still a kid at heart; she couldn't help feeling the same way when she entered her car before races—like her younger self on her birthday, loosening that last silk ribbon on each of her gifts.

One thing she'd learned over the years was that no race was like the other—she had to be prepared for anything. Lotte loved the adrenaline rush she got when she sat behind the steering wheel, which might have been one of the reasons for her success. Her house, her garden, her cars, her clothes, her social circle … all screamed *wealth*. She was proud, because what she had achieved in her twenties, most only dreamt of in their lifetime. She was living the way she'd always imagined for herself.

Everything was great.

* * *

A reporter tried to get Lotte's attention as she walked toward her racing car—the one she knew would help her cross the finish line. But instead of stopping to talk, she continued further down on the paved road, deeper into the forest that surrounded her, until the reporter was out of sight. It was quiet and a bit chilly, the calm before the storm. A crisp breeze traveled through the air occasionally, making the branches on nearby trees strike each other, blowing her hair lightly in the wind—but that was it. It was peaceful.

Every now and then, people called her selfish since she always ignored the media before races, but they would never understand how she felt. They would never understand what it was like to live the life of Lotte Jensen, winner of several world championships. Lotte Jensen, Denmark's most promising race car driver. She'd stopped counting how many times she saw herself featured in magazines, how many times she'd seen her name listed as one of the most successful people her age—a woman with a bright future ahead of her. At times it became exhausting, let alone overwhelming.

Not many understood the pressure.

She couldn't breathe easy until hers was the first car across the finish line. Winning was everything to her, since winning gave her purpose.

Nothing was going to ruin her preparation for the race.

Lotte was known for her sassy attitude; playing dirty and being a brat. Although, she always felt a stinging pain in her chest when she thought of it. It was just a shell. She would never cheat in any way or be purposely rude. Regardless, she was used to getting those types of comments, even when she made the smallest of missteps. Being one of the best, she had to swallow it, even though it made her furious when the media twisted her words and caused rumors to stick like superglue. But, as with waking up at the crack of dawn, she was used to it.

She was used to being Lotte "the Devil" Jensen.

Showing attitude was also a useful skill to have, a way to

avoid being eaten alive by the male-dominated sport. Displaying weakness in any way would never work. She had no other choice but to give them the same treatment they gave her—side-eyes and damn good racing.

Despite the downsides, Lotte did everything to maintain her career. Racing made her happy, racing was her life. It was the only thing she knew, the only thing she wanted to know.

Cheering voyaged with the wind when people began to fill the platforms further away—but nothing was going to ruin her moment of peace.

Nothing.

Instead of listening to the distant noise, she leaned against her car and set her gaze above the trees' crowns, counting the few fluffy cotton clouds covering the blue midday sky. It wasn't her first run with the Nürburgring. The Nürburgring Nordschleife in Germany was infamous for its tricky corners and terrifying route. Many people called the circuit "Green Hell," but wasn't that perfect for "the Devil?" A grin formed on her lips before she closed her eyes, took a deep breath and imagined how it would be racing through the circuit. How it would feel putting her foot on the gas pedal, turning the steering wheel with her hands and how it would feel to press her lips against the trophy after she crossed the finish line first.

Everything was great.

* * *

Lotte's dad stuck his head through her car window. In keeping with tradition, he gave her a high five, as did her mom. Before her parents disappeared into the crowd and went their separate ways, her dad waved goodbye and shouted his usual greeting for good luck, *"Held og lykke, skat!"*

Her sister, on the other hand, leaned against a wall a few meters away and gave Lotte a smile that didn't quite reach its full potential. She watched everything from a distance, wearing an orange and yellow print T-shirt with "Sunshine on my Mind" splayed across the chest.

It certainly didn't look like it.

Lykke, Lotte's younger sister, had never enjoyed racing in the same way as the rest of her family. She'd never cared to find out what racing really was about. Lotte accepted that. Just Lykke being there meant more to Lotte than her sister could ever imagine. Even though it sometimes didn't seem like it, having her family nearby was something she appreciated. At least, after the races when she could finally let her guard down and relax.

As all participants began to prepare for the race, Lotte put on one more layer of her red signature lipstick before looking through the car window next to hers. She gave the guy—who she'd spent many mornings and nights with lately—a wink and he gave her one back, before they started their engines.

Mirrors, belt, doors, no eye contact. Mirrors, belt, doors, no eye contact. Mirrors, belt, doors, no eye contact.

Lotte was known for always having her eyes glued to the road. She was known for always taking every turn with precision. She was known for always being at one with her car. People shouting, growling engines and the sound of wheels screeching against asphalt—nothing could make her look anywhere else than where she was supposed to.

Eyes on the prize.

Lotte was well aware of how important that focus was; she

knew how quickly things could go wrong and how easily her greatest skills could fail her.

Much later, her memories from the race would be vague, but she would remember her sister yelling from a distance and her mother shaking her shoulders in panic. She knew her dad was somewhere in a nearby building, in a manager's room, together with some members of her team the moment it happened. Afterward, she'd heard from others that he threw something at the TV as he watched her car drift off the track at breakneck speed.

In life, you're taught lessons and sometimes you learn them the hard way. Your life can change in a matter of days, hours, minutes or even seconds—so it's important to make use of every single second you get. You never know when your life will take a turn and change forever. You never know when it will be the last time you'll get to do the thing you love the most.

You never know.

In Lotte's case, she'd learn that winning wasn't everything.

CHAPTER ONE

"For God's sake, you can't sit here sulking any longer. It's been months!" Lotte's mom stood with her arms across her chest, urging her daughter to agree. But Lotte wasn't that easy to convince, since she was the one who'd been through hell, not her mom. Lotte doubted her mom would ever understand what she was going through.

Seeing a frown begin to form on her daughter's forehead, she continued, "I know it must be tough, skat, but you have to move on. Your dad, your sister and I, we can't continue to stand by and see you like this." The thunder in her eyes began to disappear, giving way to tears. "Please, think about other people for once, not only yourself…"

She sat down on the edge of the sofa in the living room, in her daughter's new home, bought a few months back—a house far away from memories of the past and, mostly, of Lotte's trophies. Hunching her shoulders, her mom didn't dare keep her eyes fixed on Lotte's after those words were spoken. Instead, she tilted her head downward and stared at the wooden floor.

"My whole life shattered into pieces, mom. Stop acting like you know what I'm going through!" Lotte shouted.

"Please, think about it? I can write down the number to the support group for you. Talking to people who are, or have been, in the same situation as you may do you good," her mom claimed as she stood up and walked away to go and fetch a notepad. Lotte's mom was forty-five, but nevertheless, she didn't think about the fact that she could have simply sent her daughter a text message with the details. Funny, coming from the woman who always said that things should be done in the easiest way possible. Still, her mother went on searching for the notepad, leaving her to mull over the words.

Despite being sick and tired of her constant badgering, Lotte had been debating for a while whether it would be a good idea to make one—only one—visit to that support group everyone in her family had been suggesting for weeks. She was unsure whether she'd actually be able to speak with strangers about her regrets and the day that had changed everything. Her nagging fear was that someone would judge her, laugh in her face. Many had already done just that. The thought of it sent a shiver down her spine. However, she'd never have to meet those people in person, because she would never be able to go back to racing.

As it was, she no longer had control of the lower half of her body. She couldn't feel her legs. She couldn't walk. Day in and day out she sat in a wheelchair—still the temporary kind from the hospital—which she wished would live up to its name.

Temporary.

She had tried to see things from the bright side, but it was hard to be optimistic, when even a simple thing like smiling was physically draining. Every day that passed, Lotte wished she lived in a story where she could wake up and realize everything that happened was a vivid dream. The past months, all she'd done was observe the walls around the house, lie in bed staring at the ceiling and, at times, glance at the scars—reminding herself to forget who she used to be.

When she'd understood she would never be able to race again, her whole world fell apart. She couldn't even begin to describe the wrenching ache she'd felt in her heart at that exact moment. At times, many people—her own family included—thought she was overreacting. That made her even more furious, since she had never felt so restricted.

She couldn't blame them, either. After all, it wasn't until it happened to *her* that she realized how much not being able to feel one's legs could affect someone's life. How much she couldn't do, how many things she regretted never trying, and everything that was now lost. There was nothing that could make her smile.

Nothing was good anymore.

Lotte held the piece of paper with the phone number in one hand, and her phone in the other. She looked back and forth between the two until she finally decided to dial the number. The paper in her left hand began to crumple. Her stiffened body made her hold it a bit too hard.

Since the accident she had, more or less, only interacted with her closest family members. What if she made a bad first impression on the people in the group? What if they too saw her as "the Devil?" She let herself think about it for a second, but realized that a new start maybe wouldn't be so bad after all. If they didn't like her, she could always quit.

No strings attached, that was something she was used to.

Lost in her thoughts, it slipped her mind she'd even dialed the number. She startled when she heard the gravelly voice on the other end answer, "Bernard speaking, how may I help you?"

"Oh hi, my name is Lotte ... I uh, I'm calling because I would like to join the support group. This ... is this the right number?" Bernard chuckled at her response and Lotte instantly regretted calling him. A wave of embarrassment washed over her as she realized she'd become a socially awkward introvert. She was convinced that her clammy fingertips would leave marks on the back of her phone case. She should have been more prepared.

"You're welcome to join us! I've already talked to your mother about this. We actually have a group session planned this afternoon at two o'clock if you're interested in starting today?"

Lotte was used to planning everything in her life, from the minute she woke up to the minute she closed her eyelids for the day. She wasn't the biggest fan of any quick change in plans, but she really didn't have anything important to do that day, or any day, since the accident. Going would make her family, especially her mom, proud. The disappointment in her mother's eyes was something she couldn't bear to see for one more day. Despite that, Lotte rolled her eyes when Bernard told her that she'd already been in contact with him.

Of course she had.

Deep down she understood why; she knew her mom was only trying to help her. "Yes, that sounds ... That sounds great. I-I hope it's okay with the other group members?" Lotte asked.

"Oh, don't worry about that, I'm sure Nova, Ian and Kenley will appreciate seeing a new face around here," he assured her.

After hanging up the phone, her spirits rose. Her heart sped up with relief, easing her inner demons a bit. She put her phone on her lap and looked down at her split ends and the worn out pajama pants she'd basically been living in lately—something that was visible due to the stains. It was probably her sign to finally get rid of both.

After lunch, they rode down to the city center where she asked to be dropped off a block away from the address Bernard had given them. Since her mom was an expert in how to make situations awkward, she chose to make the final trek alone.

The clock was about to strike two and Lotte still hadn't arrived at the address. She sat completely still in her wheelchair on the sidewalk, surrounded by trees, traffic lights and stores with big display windows. As she watched people pass her by, she couldn't help thinking about how much each person took for granted in being able to walk without a care in the world. The same went for the two children who ran across the street. Her mind traveled back to memories she didn't want to remember, at least not now. Like how it felt to run around on the beach that sunny day a year ago, or how it felt to put her foot on the gas pedal.

She had better start getting used to it; she was about to join a support group after all. They were supposed to talk about their issues and share their experiences with one another.

She loosened what had turned into a tight grip around the cool surface of the gray pushrims, making her knuckles regain their color, before taking a deep breath and proceeding to move forward.

* * *

"Let's wait a few more minutes, it's only ten past two after all! She should be here any minute now," Bernard said, as he put his phone back into his pocket and sat down in his chair.

A few seconds later, Lotte entered the room. She apologized and gave everyone in the room what she hoped was a warm smile. When she'd been out in the corridor, she could hear them all talking and laughing, but as soon as she'd come into the room, the laughter died and she could feel the familiar awkward feeling wash over her once again.

"Everyone, let's welcome Lotte to our group!" said the man who sounded very much like the voice from the phone earlier. *Bernard,* if she remembered it right. He was way older than the other three strangers in the room. His grayish hair was sticking out from under his hat, accompanied by a beard the same color. Covered in wrinkles, his face looked rather tired, made noticeable by his sunken eyes. But his smile was warm and welcoming, even though he had a tooth or three missing.

After a few seconds of silence he added, "So, maybe the three of you could introduce yourselves?"

The woman who sat next to him nodded her head at what he said. "I'm Nova!" she said, beaming at Lotte, like she could feel the awkward tension lingering in the room and wanted to make her feel better about the situation.

Nova was in her late twenties and she loved horses more than life itself. She had a picture-perfect smile; wide and wonderful and enough to put anyone at ease. She was beautiful, with wavy hair, big eyes and flawless skin and she had a sense for fashion that Lotte envied. Everything seemed bright on the outside, but Lotte wondered if there was more than met the eye, hidden within her. She immediately thought the same about the others in the room.

They all had shells.

A guy who looked like one of those typical heartthrobs you saw on TV and read about in books sat on the other side of Bernard. "Woah, a new member? That doesn't happen too often! I'm Ian," he said.

Lotte was certain she wasn't the only one who couldn't stop staring at his incredible ice-blue eyes and admiring that sharp jawline of his. He looked great—and so did Nova. They didn't look broken as far as she could see.

For whatever reason, Lotte searched for scars on both Nova's and Ian's faces, but she failed to find any. Lotte herself had a tiny scar on her right cheek. It was like she was looking for anything in them that she could relate to—because when you can relate to someone, or have something in common, it's easier to build up a strong relationship. She didn't want to admit it, but she was alone. All her "friends" were long gone.

"The short version—I'm a twenty-seven year old who loves

puppies and likes to watch superhero movies above anything else. So, if you ever want to discuss a movie, hit me up," Ian offered, winking at her. She tried her best not to think about her cheeks heating up.

"He's obsessed! He's *that* person who talks non-stop during movies. Annoying, right?" Nova added playfully.

Ian sighed loudly, turning away from Nova. After a while though, he beamed back at her, almost as if he couldn't stop himself.

Lotte turned to the last person in the room.

Kendrick? Kevin?

She smiled at the man whose name she'd forgotten, but he didn't smile back. Maybe he was one of those people who hated when people were late? Or maybe she'd accidentally done something to offend him? Instantly the overthinking started and she tried to figure out where it could have gone wrong, before it was just as quickly interrupted.

"I'm Kenley," he said, his lips curving into some sort of half-smile as he turned toward Bernard, giving him a look like he wanted him to continue, but didn't have the words.

Kenley wore a blue jean jacket over a white shirt, together with a pair of black ripped jeans. He had a watch on his wrist, wore a pair of vintage-looking glasses, his white sneakers appeared almost new, and the dark curls on his head were perfectly combed.

A mix between comfort and style.

He didn't mention his age, but it looked like he was around the same age as Lotte. Somewhere in his early- or mid-twenties.

Kenley faced Lotte again and broke the silence by saying, "So, can I ask why you're here, Lotte?"

She froze, taken aback. Her lips parted, but no words came out. He refused to share anything about himself and instead he asked her the most *obvious* question ever. She frowned and snapped, "What does it look like? Take a look for yourself!"

It came out of her mouth a bit more aggressively than she'd intended and she realized right away that it might have been a very bad move. She was just so used to having to defend herself —defend every single movement and decision she made. That, and being constantly reminded that she now was a wheelchair user, was something she couldn't bear any longer.

Lotte glanced at Nova and Ian, whose friendly and welcoming smiles had now been replaced with rather worried faces. Their eyes darted from Lotte to Kenley and then back again, almost in sync.

Kenley leaned forward and rested his forearms on his legs. He wasn't expecting a response like that to come from someone who seemed to be shy and soft-spoken. At least, that had been his first impression of her, based only on hearing her say a few words. His grin spread from ear to ear and after a moment of silence he said, "That might be a bit difficult to do, since I'm nearly completely blind."

CHAPTER TWO

She had one job and that was not to embarrass herself during the first meeting. But what did she do? She told an near-blind man to look at her. Lotte could feel her cheeks flush red and she didn't dare to look up to face anyone in the room.

"It's fine. I know it's not really visible," he assured her, in an attempt to make her feel better about the situation.

Lotte looked up from the floor for the first time in what seemed like an eternity and met his eyes. That was true. At a glance, his eyes looked completely unaffected and there was no cane in sight.

He had a shell, like the others.

She cleared her throat and said, "I'm sorry, that came out the wrong way, I ..." But it was at that same moment she saw it—a tiny scar on his chin. She immediately wanted to know more about it, because it looked a lot like hers. Instead, keeping her mouth shut after her outburst a minute earlier seemed like a much better plan.

The rest of the session, Bernard shared stories about his life, mainly about his kids and grandkids. How one time, his granddaughter had eaten so many strawberries he feared she would explode. How his grandson had jumped on his butt instead of crawling like most babies did. The way his daughter used to collect wads of chewing gum under the sofa instead of throwing them in the trash can. How he'd proposed to his wife with a candy ring. He shared so many wholesome stories with the group that his life started to sound like a romantic comedy.

Apart from creating an environment where sharing their deepest struggles could be accepted and their voices heard, he also managed to show them how significant the *little things* in life were to find happiness. How important it was to bring them into the light, even though they often got run over by the memories too difficult to shake.

It didn't seem like the first time Nova, Ian and Kenley had heard Bernard's stories, yet they hung on his every word. Lotte, on the other hand, was lost in a world of her own thoughts for the rest of the session and when she was asked questions, she kept her answers short. Her shell wasn't hard to break these days, and she would prefer not to have an emotional breakdown in front of strangers, new friends or not.

Later in the afternoon the sun had started to set, signaling it was time to go home, at least for Nova and Ian. They waved at Lotte before they walked out of the building. She followed them with her eyes through the window and saw them stop across the street, admiring the pink and yellow sky, before continuing to walk until they were out of sight.

Lotte's parents were running errands, but her mom had promised to pick her up as soon as they were done, so she knew she'd probably have to wait in the building for a while.

Something she longed for was freedom. Most of the time, she had to rely on others. She missed how she used to be able to drive away in her car, without having to tell anyone where she was going, or who she was with.

Something the crash had taken away from her.

Lotte tried once again to close the doors to her dream land—it wasn't worth thinking impossible things. Turning her chair around, she saw Kenley sitting on a sofa at the other end of the big reception area. It was so silent you could probably hear a pin drop. Lotte watched as he gazed at the marble floor with the same passion she applied to staring at the wooden ceiling in her room. A cane was leaning against his leg, like he was waiting for some sort of signal to stand up and leave the building.

But as the minutes passed, he still sat in the same position, on the same sofa, waiting for something. Lotte went back and forth wondering if she should move from her spot and try to start a conversation with him. She knew it could possibly cause more trouble, but it was a chance to apologize, since she felt like her attempt earlier was half-hearted. Which was why, after a lot of deliberating, she went over to him.

"Hey, Kenley, right?" Lotte looked at him, trying to force a smile onto her lips, before the cane next to him reminded her that he couldn't see it. Her cheeks heated up after realizing she approached him like she didn't know his name. She knew it pretty well by now. It was the only thing that had been on her mind the past few hours. "What are you going to do now? Are you waiting for someone?" she asked, her voice coming out a bit more confident.

"I'm waiting for my mom. She's supposed to pick me up, but it seems like I might be stuck here for a while," he sighed, tilting his head down.

"I'm actually waiting for my mom too, so maybe we can keep each other company?" Lotte thought that was the least she could do for him after what happened earlier. "Do you live far from here?" she asked.

Kenley shook his head. "No, only a few minutes away. But you know, this whole 'no vision' thing is still kind of new to me. I have a lot to learn when it comes to walking in traffic …"

"Let me be your eyes then?" Lotte blurted out. In the midst of saying it, she began to doubt whether it was something he would actually agree to. They'd only known each other for a couple of hours and the first thing she did when they met was imply that he was a sighted person. For a second, she forgot about the cars and other hazards of a busy city.

From the look on his face, she was certain he'd try to figure out a way to politely decline her proposal. Instead, he surprised her by saying, "If you want to, and have the time, I would be glad for you to help me home."

"Are you sure?"

"I've had to learn to put a lot of trust in people. So actually, it would be really nice of you," he assured.

"Okay, just give me the address." She tried her best to give him her most genuine smile—which she once again reminded herself he couldn't see—as he stood up, folded his cane and grasped the handles of her wheelchair. Then they went out of the building—Lotte as his new set of eyes.

"What does it look like?" Kenley asked. He stopped walking and was now standing still on a bridge in the middle of the city, his hands resting on her chair. "I'm pretty sure that's water I hear?"

Lotte nodded approvingly, but it took her a few seconds once again to realize that he couldn't see her bobbing head. *Remember to use your words*, she thought to herself.

"It is. The water reflects the sunbeams in such a beautiful way, looking almost light pink, with a touch of purple and orange. Like the sky right now," she said. She wondered whether it was wrong of her to call things beautiful; things he might never be able to see with his own eyes again. She imagined living in a world where she couldn't see—all the colors and all the things happening around her.

Kenley let go of the handles of her wheelchair and took a step forward. "Tell me more." He stood next to her and fixed his eyes in the direction of the small river that was flowing through the city. He could glimpse some sort of glow next to them, probably a streetlight, but what he couldn't know, until Lotte told him, was that it was old fashioned and weather-beaten.

The bridge was a little over a hundred years old. Kenley could hear the old wooden planks creak a bit under his feet and feel the coldness of the steel on the bridge railing with his hand. A gust of wind caressed his cheeks and he could smell the scent of newly baked muffins and pies. Lotte told Kenley there was a bakery at the end of the bridge and that they definitely had to visit it sometime—her treat.

She herself was stunned that such a proposal had come out of her mouth. Since when was she the one who wanted to hang out? Instead of sitting at home, alone, as she had done for most of the past months.

The rest of the time they shared on the bridge, she continued to amplify Kenley's imaginary picture of what the surroundings looked like. For instance, that the wooden planks were taupe, that the bridge's wires were a shade of bronze and how tiny the massive buildings on the other side of the river looked from where they stood.

Lotte had a way with words, and for the first time in a long while, he could see things—or at least, something almost as good. He could picture what the landscape she described looked like; something no one had succeeded in doing so far.

Kenley had moved to the city a few months earlier and hadn't yet seen the city with his own eyes. No one ever really managed to describe to him what they saw either. While some actually did try, their colorless explanations didn't make him want to know more. They were boring, gray and meaningless.

"Can you see me?" Lotte asked, leaning with her arms on the fencing and looking up at Kenley who at the same moment turned his head in her direction.

"I can see the contours of you, but not *you*," he said, in a low tone. "But I bet you are very beautiful!" he added shortly after, before he realized it may have come off the wrong way. He breathed a sigh of relief when he heard her giggling next to him.

Lotte rested her head on her arms again, as she watched the sunset with Kenley next to her, describing all the things she could see—even the tiny details.

As they arrived outside his apartment building, the sun had almost gone down completely. The two of them had stayed at the bridge for longer than expected and taken a detour around the city—all to let the moment last a little longer.

"You seem like someone I can trust, Lotte. Maybe you could help me out again some time?" he asked.

She never believed her evening would end up like it did; she thought they, especially Kenley, would keep their distance after the session. "Of course," she said, before adding, "I would love that." The last part came out of her mouth more like a whisper, a whisper she wasn't sure he heard because of the cars passing by on the road next to them. She rested her elbow on the armrest of her wheelchair, but after a few seconds she shifted to the other side instead, not really knowing what to do or where to place her arms and hands.

Both of them tried to manage their lives and face all the struggles that came their way. Lotte imagined it would do her good to spend time with someone like him, someone who could relate. Maybe joining the support group hadn't been such a bad idea after all. Because what she felt that evening was a bit of hope, at least a glimpse of it—especially during those few seconds when he beamed at her.

He radiated sunshine.

She had to admit, he was attractive. It was something about his smile, those tiny dimples that came with it and the small gap between his front teeth. It was something about how the setting sun made his umber brown skin shine when they were on the bridge. It was something about his style, his confident yet still somewhat awkward aura and, *oh*, she couldn't forget his glasses.

Lotte wanted to get to know him more, even the things most people tried to avoid talking about. If he ended up telling her his story, she wanted to be there for him, the way she wished her friends could have been there for her. Feeling curious, she debated whether it was too soon to ask him right away. When it came to racing, curiosity was a good quality to have. She'd yet to discover whether it applied to this new world of hers.

"You told me all this was kind of new to you. How long have you been without vision?" she asked.

Kenley, who stood a couple of meters in front of her, took a deep breath. "It happened a few months ago. I don't think I should say anything more at the moment, that would ... kill the mood of this beautiful evening." His voice became a bit shaky as he tried to form some sort of smile to cover the pain she had reminded him of.

"Oh, sorry if I ..."

"It's fine. See you next week!" Kenley said, hurrying to turn away from her.

Lotte waited outside on the sidewalk until she saw the door close behind him. She hadn't realized it until then, but for the first time in months, she had smiled—a sort of genuine smile. And for the first time in months, she found herself longing for something.

She longed for the next session.

* * *

"Who the hell is *Lotta*?" Kenley's mom said. Dressed in stiff, black-and-white business clothes, she burst into the kitchen with her coat hanging over her one arm and her worn-out loafers in the other hand, after she overheard pieces of a conversation between Kenley and her sister, Fajah. A few strands from her curly dark brown hair fell out from behind her ear and covered parts of her face as she hurried into the room.

"A very thoughtful woman, *Lotte*, helped me home," Kenley said, turning to her. "Which I'm really thankful for. Seems like once again, you forgot you were supposed to pick me up!?" He'd always been good at keeping his calm, it was rare for him to raise his voice at his mother, but something inside of him snapped.

"Shit Kenny … I thought your dad …" She didn't finish the sentence. She knew she'd already used all the excuses in the book and that no matter what she said, it wouldn't help the situation. Her mood shifted for a split second before she remembered why she stormed into the kitchen in the first place. "So, who is she?"

"Delilah, come on! Let the guy be!" Fajah glanced at her sister and sighed. She knew that Delilah was very overprotective of her son, but at this point it was starting to annoy Fajah. She was well aware that she was worried—everything had changed *that* day, even though they rarely spoke of it. But all Fajah wanted for Kenley was for him to keep living his life.

His mom made it hard.

Kenley had struggled with a lot of things these past months, so to see his face light up a bit when he talked about this young woman who helped him home, almost made her heart skip a beat.

He wasn't Fajah's son, she was just his aunt, but in her eyes, he had always been her little boy.

"She's a new member of the support group," Kenley answered after a moment of complete silence.

Delilah's eyes narrowed. "Okay, and who is she to you?" she asked in a firm, almost harsh voice.

"You know what, mom? Why don't you keep minding your own business, like you've done the whole day?"

Delilah got a bit offended by his reply and said, "You know I only have one son. I don't want—" Kenley tightened his jaw and narrowed his eyes in the direction of his mother, which made her stumble on her words. She just couldn't help it, especially not after she'd already spent too many hours at work; her mind was drained. She wished she could tell Kenley the truth, but it was difficult finding a way to tell him that she was struggling to pay off his debts. Delilah knew it would only make her son furious.

"It's the past. Can we just forget about it?" he pleaded.

"Okay you two, enough with the sad faces!" Fajah bumped her elbow against Kenley's arm with a smirk and said, "Tell me more about the girl!"

CHAPTER THREE

Shortly after Kenley went inside his apartment building that evening, Lotte's mom came to pick her up. She helped Lotte into the car, put the wheelchair in the back and, as expected, asked her daughter a million questions. It had been a long day; Lotte's eyelids became heavier and heavier, she just didn't have the energy.

Resting her head in the palm of her hand, she leaned against the passenger door while looking out of the window. It occurred to her that the accident had barely crossed her mind for two whole hours. Those thoughts had been replaced by something much more interesting, something she would much rather think about.

It wasn't until they drove past a city sign indicating the exit, to the place where the only car she had left was parked, that everything began haunting her mind once more. Her heart rate increased, thinking about how everything had gone so wrong.

Even though she knew she might never be able to feel her legs again, she had saved her favorite car, just in case. Edward, an old family friend, owned a big garage where people could rent a spot for their beloved vehicles if they didn't have enough room themselves. Lotte did have a lot of space, in fact, she had four empty garages at her current home. She just couldn't bear seeing it day in and day out.

Some days, when she felt ready to burst from all the tears she refused to let fall, taking a taxi to visit Edward's garage was just what she needed. There she could cry out alone, in peace, inside her car, despite her parents' disapproval. She was lucky Edward didn't tell them everything. It was their secret that she showed up there sometimes, when her parents thought she was visiting a friend who actually didn't exist. It gave her the adrenaline rush she had missed so immensely.

* * *

About a week had passed since the group's last session. Nova and Kenley were a bit early, so they waited outside the building in the morning sun for Bernard and the rest of the group to arrive. "So, you and Lotte, huh?" Nova asked, eagerly waiting for a reply, but Kenley had zoned out. "Earth to Kenley Kimathi?"

Nova had been talking about a trip she'd planned for five minutes straight. Kenley was exhausted and lost in his own thoughts. His mind was all over the place; he wasn't paying much attention to what she said. The previous day, he'd spent several hours at the hospital, sitting next to someone who seemed to be more dead than alive. He didn't notice Nova changing the subject.

"Huh?" was the only thing he managed to get out of his mouth.

"Bernie told me he saw you and Lotte leave the building together last week. Is that true? Oh, my life is so freaking boring, give me all the tea!" she squealed. Without even being able to see, Kenley knew Nova would be looking at him, eyes wide, eager to know more.

Kenley cleared his throat and carried on folding his cane.

"She just helped me home." He hoped that was enough of an answer for Nova and that she would hopefully change the subject after that—but no. Nova was curious; she asked him if Lotte told him anything about herself, like what had happened to her. He shook his head no; she didn't tell him much. Asking right away wasn't really an option either. Kenley knew what it felt like to be asked about something he'd rather not talk about. He knew that Lotte would tell him sooner or later, when she felt comfortable enough to do so. He could tell it was a sensitive subject for her to open up about.

"Lotte Jensen, many articles to read," she said. Nova inhaled some of the fresh morning air as she grabbed Kenley by his arm and started to walk toward the entrance of the building. *Of course* she'd decided to look it up herself. A part of him didn't want to know, but another part couldn't take the suspense that sentence held.

"She is—I mean, she was, a racer. You know, with cars and stuff."

For a few seconds he could feel his heart ache for her. He thought of the pain he'd been going through himself, both mentally and physically. The type of pain that you *know* more people must be feeling, but you still hope they don't. In his mind, he could picture a wrecked car, a woman lying unconscious on the ground, flames, smoke, blood, dust, screaming.

Déjà vu.

Kenley tried to erase those pictures from his mind; it wasn't a good time to remember.

"Have you told Lotte about ... *you know?*" Nova asked as she opened the door to the building so they could walk inside.

"We don't know each other that well. We only hung out for about two hours. She's still kind of a stranger to me," he said as he walked inside. Kenley tried to keep a straight face but it was hard, because he knew very well he wanted to get to know that stranger more. But the question was whether he would be walking on dangerous ground if he did.

"Two hours? Don't you live like ten minutes away from here or something, hm?" she asked, leaning closer, to make sure she could read every single small movement his face made. Knowing Kenley preferred to be alone, it came as a surprise that he spent two hours with a woman who'd made a less-than-stellar first impression on him. That meant there must be more to the story than he was telling her. Nova hadn't known Kenley for long, but she knew him well enough to see when he was trying to hide a smile. Enough to know that he was thinking of the woman who'd made an almost completely blind man open his eyes for the first time in months.

All five of them were sitting in a circle in the small room inside the big building, like the previous week. Once again, Lotte was greeted by friendly smiles—something she wasn't used to, but wouldn't mind becoming familiar with. Being afraid the awkward tension would still linger in the room, she was relieved when it appeared like the troublesome happenings from the previous week's session were erased from their minds.

"So, Lotte, do you want to start with telling us something, anything, you have experienced this last week?" Bernard asked while he adjusted his hat.

"Nothing special I can remember now," Lotte sighed.

"Not even one little thing?" Bernard asked, trying his best to get some sort of positive answer out of her. But it was hard when her default setting was negativity. The truth was, Lotte had hung out with her parents, she'd baked a cake or two and had read several books, annotating as she went. But nothing could compare to the things she used to do before the crash. What she'd done in the past week was the same as the weeks before that—it was nothing new, nothing exciting.

"My life shattered into pieces when I found out I'd never be able to race again. Racing meant everything to me—still does. It was like all happiness, all hope, all my dreams disappeared in the blink of an eye," Lotte explained, feeling the lump in her throat growing bigger. She could sense everyone holding their breath and she didn't dare look up from the floor. It was important everyone knew how she felt; she was tired of being told to look at life on the bright side. She was especially tired of hearing it from people who could walk.

Lotte was aware of the people out there that had it much worse than her, but she couldn't help feeling sorry for herself. She'd lost everything—her whole career—in a matter of seconds.

But there was more to the story, something only she knew.

Lotte bit her lower lip and wondered if it was a good idea to continue, since she could already feel the atmosphere becoming heavy and her heart slowly being torn apart. Yet, she didn't hold back when she said, "The accident ... it's haunting me."

Feeling her eyes tear up and her throat become dry, she glanced to her right in the hope of receiving some sort of comfort from the only person she knew a little bit better than the rest in the room—Kenley. She knew he couldn't see her, but he didn't even look up. Instead he fiddled with the sleeve on his jacket, like he wasn't listening at all.

Kenley was the type of person who could stay focused for hours straight, but during this specific session, his mind wandered to other planets as he tried to figure out how to make this sad woman smile—genuinely. He knew that telling her to move on wouldn't work, since letting go of such heavy things took time—especially if she'd lost the only thing keeping her dreams alive.

Kenley wanted more than anything to show her that she could

be happy again. He wanted to show her that it was possible to live a full life.

Racing excluded.

***

After the session, Lotte found herself once again sitting in the lobby, observing things and people around her. A few raindrops on the window next to her caught her attention. It was like the raindrops were having a race, making her wonder which one of them would reach the ground first. The raindrops that stayed on the glass the longest would keep their shape and form. They wouldn't only be part of a small meaningless puddle on the ground as the rest.

Sometimes winning wasn't everything.

"What you told us today was really moving," Kenley said, approaching her from behind.

She quickly turned around when she heard his voice. It seemed like he'd been listening to some of what she said after all.

"I know life can be a pain in the ass sometimes, but it doesn't mean it's the end, you can still do a lot!" He started searching for the sofa he'd been told was somewhere nearby with his cane, following the sound of her voice. When he sat down, he beamed at her.

"Like what?" she asked, sounding very doubtful. Lotte half expected what he would say next, since many people had already tried to get her back on her feet, not only literally.

"Let me show you!"

"When and where? Sorry, I'm used to planning everything …"

"Can I get your number? Maybe I can call you later today?"

"Oh, yeah, s-sure! My number is—" she broke off, and before she could keep going, he handed his phone to her.

"Can you please type it in for me?" he asked.

It almost made Lotte blush that she had once again seemed to take a lot of things for granted. He could see the contours of her, but not much more than that. So how was he supposed to see the screen of his phone?

"There you go," she said, handing it back to him.

"Great, I might already have something planned for tonight. I'll call you."

Lotte couldn't help feeling a bit anxious. It was always a challenge going to unknown places with her wheelchair. Going somewhere with a blind man wouldn't make it any easier—at least, so she thought. He'd told her not even a week earlier that he'd learned to put a lot of trust in people, even the ones he didn't know well. He trusted her to be his eyes. Now it was time for her to trust him with whatever he had planned.

※ ※ ※

"Oh, count me in! I'm going to race until the day I die!" cried a cheerful and delighted Lotte to a reporter, as she held a massive golden trophy in her hands. Then the video cut back to a newscaster, who told the story of what had happened that Sunday in May at ten past two in the afternoon.

Kenley couldn't see what was happening on his computer screen, but he could hear her voice. It was almost like he wanted to believe it was another person at first; her tone was completely different. It was the way she described racing—like it was the most precious jewel. She had a flourishing career, she was doing something she loved, she was happy and clearly not at all prepared for how fast things would change for her.

When Kenley was at his worst, the only person he felt like he could rely on fully was Fajah. It was no use even trying to start a conversation with his mom. On top of that, his dad had been away at the time and not many of his friends knew how to handle the new and unusual situation they'd been put in. He knew what it felt like to be at rock bottom; he wished that some people around him would have reacted differently, so he could have had more than one shoulder to cry on. That was another reason why he couldn't get Lotte off his mind; he knew that he could help her—at least in some way. Kenley remembered how many times he'd wanted someone to come into his life to save him from the pain. Maybe he wouldn't be able to take it all away from her, but he hoped to, at least, shorten the grieving process.

Fajah opened the door and peeked in, head first. "Hey Kenny! You wanted to walk the last bit on your own, right? We'll have to leave now, we can't let your girl wait for too long!"

Kenley nodded and smiled at the fact that Fajah called Lotte *his girl*. It wasn't a date, just an act of kindness. He and Lotte were friends, or at least almost friends. But he didn't correct his aunt, since Fajah was thrilled—something she hadn't been in a while. It made Kenley's heart feel warm, like some light of the sun that used to be there, slowly returned.

At the same time as Kenley tied his shoelaces in Fajah's apartment, Lotte was at home trying to decide what to wear. She had no idea what they were going to do that evening, so she thought it was a good idea to go with something she felt comfortable wearing, like a pair of linen pants and a simple T-shirt, which also was something she'd learned to put on herself. Jeans and other tight-fitting clothes were always a challenge for her, which she didn't have time for at that moment.

Something she also always kept in mind on those few occasions when she left her home, was to wear clothes that covered her worst scars and other permanent marks.

Before she went outside she quickly grabbed her jacket and handbag and waved her parents goodbye. It was a sight they weren't used to. They'd lived with Lotte for months, but it wasn't often she went out willingly.

As the door was closing, she could hear her mom whispering about how proud she was of her daughter and what a beautiful woman she had become, despite everything that had happened. Her dad on the other hand said he wasn't surprised; Lotte had his amazing genes after all! At that, her mom muttered something under her breath with a sly grin.

Lotte waited for Kenley in the evening sunlight outside her stone mansion and though she tried her best, she couldn't stop herself from glancing at her phone every other second. He was ten minutes late. Deep inside she knew she wasn't being stood up, but her past experiences with guys didn't help the situation.

In the past, she'd fallen for men who showed the same dreamy, heavenly gaze they showed her, to other women at the same time. Months, and years, later she still wondered what made her interested in them in the first place. Her logical brain screamed no, but for some reason the opposite always managed to come out of her mouth. Probably because she wanted that 'happy ever after' so badly. She'd definitely learned a lot of things the hard way.

When she looked over her shoulder, she could see Kenley further down the street trying to navigate his way through all the enormous flower pots one of her neighbors had placed on the sidewalk. He moved his cane slowly from left to right, right to left, as he got closer to her. Her street was new to him and he wasn't familiar with the surroundings like he was around his own area—he found it a bit nerve-racking to walk in unknown territory.

Through the haze that covered his vision, he could just about see the contours of someone in front of him. "Sorry I'm late!" he said, hoping it was Lotte in front of him on the sidewalk.

She tried to force a smile onto her lips to reassure him, but how was he supposed to *hear* that? A moment later, she ended up saying: "Oh, it's fine. You're here now!"

He sighed and folded his cane. "I hope you didn't have to wait here for too long."

It was then that Lotte noticed there was no one else in sight. "Did you ... Did you walk here by yourself?"

Kenley shook his head. "My aunt dropped me off down the street. I wanted to try to walk the last meters up to your doorstep myself. It's not long, but at least it's something."

Her eyes widened. "Really? That's amazing!"

He wished she could see her own progress the same way.

"Everything is possible, sometimes it just takes time," he said. "Sometimes you have to take one day at a time, brick by brick, in order to achieve something great in the end."

His words made Lotte think twice—she knew he was right. It was just hard for her to realize that not everything had a quick fix; that her bank account or her name couldn't fix all of her problems.

"So, what do you have planned for tonight?" she asked, trying to change the subject, feeling the tension grow stronger.

"I'm taking you to an amusement park!" Kenley exclaimed. He must have known pretty damn well how she would react, even though he hadn't known her for long. He tried to hide a grin forming on his lips.

Lotte had imagined a lot of scenarios, but she hadn't let her imagination travel *that* far. She never believed she'd visit an amusement park so soon, and she definitely didn't expect that a blind man would be the one to take her.

Moving closer, he said, "There are still so many things we can do. Just let me show you."

CHAPTER FOUR

The sun had slowly started to set as they arrived, with Fajah behind the wheel, and Lotte had to admit that the place looked tempting. The colors of the approaching night sky fit well together with the amusement park's rich collection of twinkling lights, and the cents of cotton candy and freshly baked buns filled the air. It brought back blissful memories from Lotte's childhood, like when she and Lykke visited Tivoli in Copenhagen for the first time.

The only thing that made her doubt Kenley's choice of place after seeing it, was that all the people who had come through the gate had two functioning legs. Specifically, a bunch of kids she saw pretty much dancing past them, couples walking in front of them while holding hands and friends running into each other's arms in greeting.

"You do realize I can't feel my legs, right?" she said as she looked up at Kenley standing beside her.

"You know it's called an *amusement* park, not a rollercoaster park, right?" he asked, grinning, before starting to push her wheelchair into the park, following her directions.

About a year earlier, when she visited an amusement park

with her former friends, the only thing they'd done was look for anything that could give them an adrenaline rush, make their blood pump and give them goosebumps—not unlike the effect racing had on her. Lotte had never even glanced at the arcade area before; all the cafés, the restaurants, the decorations and the park itself were bursting with life. It was like Kenley had opened up a whole new world for her, or at least, let her into a world she'd once ignored. For what felt like the first time in her life, Lotte saw things from another perspective.

He was showing her colors and shades she'd never seen before.

They could hear loud party music playing from afar and Lotte could see a cluster of neon lights further down the street. It was probably the place with all the arcade games, since many people were walking away from the area with stuffed animals in their hands.

Kenley stopped walking, trying to figure out why Lotte had been silent for the past minute. "Like what you see?"

"Oh, I'm ... admiring the view I guess?" she confessed, with an almost trembling voice. "It was a long time ago I did anything like this."

"So, what do you want to do first?" Kenley asked, as though he thought Lotte had already come up with a long list of things to do.

"Oh, I don't know," she answered, hoping Kenley wouldn't think she was too boring already.

"There's a café close by that has some really tasty cakes. We can also take a stroll in the park if you want? And don't forget all the fun games you can find around here!" He was truly trying his best, which made Lotte feel a bit guilty, since she made everything much harder by being so closed-off. She wished it would be easier to let loose, at least for a short while.

Lotte took a deep breath and said, "Maybe we can try to win a teddy bear or something? I can see a few from here." Her back was against him, so she couldn't see his reaction, but his face lit up, knowing things were heading in the right direction.

"Do you want to be my eyes then?"

* * *

"A little bit to the left!" Lotte squealed. "Stop right there! Now down!" If she could, she would for sure have jumped up and down with excitement. Lotte quickly grabbed the soft light brown plush animal that tumbled down the dispenser of the claw game. It had a white belly, a pink nose and its left ear was a bit frayed. It might have just been a bunny, but to Lotte it was the cutest stuffed thing with long ears she'd ever seen. She was excited to win something, when lately all she could remember had been how it felt to lose.

Kenley could have sworn that he'd heard her sweet laugh a minute earlier, despite the sounds from the arcade around them. He tried to focus, in the hope of seeing her eyes, her smile, her laugh lines—her something, her anything. But no matter how hard he tried, he couldn't see past that blurry, foggy wall. After being silent for a moment, he asked, "What do you say about celebrating our win with some cake?"

The corner of Lotte's mouth twitched upwards as she said, "Sure, why not?"

After only being there half an hour, she had laughed more than she'd done in the past months all together. Her muscles almost cramped from it. Everything with Kenley felt so natural.

When they sat down to eat cake at one of the cafés, it was like they were two old friends catching up after years lost. Ever since the accident, she'd neglected the feeling of joy. But being around him, she could feel her lips curving into a smile without really thinking about it. He had the same terrible sense of humor as her, and he was a good listener. The latter was something many people in her life had failed at since her accident. As night began to fall over the city, she couldn't keep from admiring his cute exterior.

On top of that, he didn't judge her because of her wheelchair. He didn't judge her because of her looks either, since he had no clue what she looked like. It was refreshing for a woman who was so used to having all eyes on her.

Since the day Kenley lost his vision, he'd been afraid to get close to people again. Afraid to hurt them. But with Lotte, it was almost impossible; it was impossible not to like her and not to want to be closer to her, which deep inside made him feel a bit worried, thinking of the mess he was in.

To Lotte it seemed like Kenley had most of his life sorted out. But, he was fighting his own demons day and night. Especially during the nights when he was completely alone in the darkness, when everything was quiet, when all he could think of were things he couldn't change and words he couldn't take back. To Kenley, Lotte was a breath of fresh air. She didn't know everything about his life yet, and therefore she couldn't judge him the way others did.

After staying at the café for over an hour, Kenley wanted to make sure there was enough time for Lotte to look at all the beautiful light decorations before they headed toward the exit. Kenley could only catch a glimpse of the countless blurry, shiny dots in the air, but thanks to Lotte, he didn't even need to have his eyes open.

What she told him was more appealing than what he could ever see.

Lotte thought to herself whether she should ask him to hang out again sometime. Or, was it too much to ask for? Maybe it was only a one-time thing? She hoped not, because she'd rather stay there with him for a while longer, than to go home and stare at the ceiling in her room, alone.

"Do you maybe want to hang out again?" Lotte blurted, hoping it wouldn't sound too desperate.

"I'd gladly ..." he started, before exhaling deeply at the end of the sentence, making Lotte sense a 'but' coming. "I just need to clear the air about something. You know, sometimes you do things that you'll end up regretting for the rest of your life." He put his hand in the pockets of his jean jacket, since it had begun to get a bit chilly, before he continued, "I had an accident a while ago. Let's just say it scarred me deeply. It made me keep my distance from a lot of people around me ... and stuff."

Instantly, Lotte felt her own scars open and she could almost feel blood running down her skin. She looked up at Kenley, hoping to meet his eyes, but he kept his gaze locked on the stone slabs under his feet, standing there in silence, like his pain had resurfaced too.

She could feel her heart crumble for him.

"I-I'm here for you if you want to talk about ... *it*," was the only thing that managed to make its way through her trembling lips. The lump in her throat made it come out as a whisper.

"I didn't only hurt myself that day, Lotte." His voice wasn't steady any longer; it was heavy with tears. "My girlfriend, she ... she ..."

Died?

Death was the first thing that came to Lotte's mind. She knew how fragile life was, how easy things could go wrong, how close she herself had been to not making it. Kenley's glossy eyes, the tears running down his face, and him not daring to finish the sentence, was strengthening her theory.

"Sorry that I brought it up," he said, wiping several small droplets away from his cheeks.

"No, I'm sorry. I'm sorry I—" Lotte replied before cutting herself off, at a loss for words.

Kenley had learned how to keep his feelings to himself and how to put on a brave face in public. At first he was shocked at how fast he fell apart, how close he was to falling to his knees in front of her. But deep down he knew that Lotte wouldn't judge him, that she wouldn't have that judgemental tone in her voice he had become too familiar with lately. She was the only one he'd met who had been through something similar—probably the reason behind why he felt comfortable around her and let himself be vulnerable. She didn't say anything when Kenley tried to pull himself together; she knew what it felt like when people time after time told her that everything was going to be okay. She listened, just listened, and took in every word that left his lips.

After a while, Kenley cleared his throat. "It's starting to get a bit chilly. We can always go to my place if you want to, while we wait for your dad. It's not far from here. And I apologize for—"

Lotte grabbed his hand and gave it a squeeze. "It's fine, no need to apologize." Then they made their way toward the exit.

The night was for sure a rollercoaster of emotions.

* * *

Kenley had moved in with his mom because of his current circumstances, he told her, seemingly embarrassed at first, from all the mumbling and unsure words that came out of his mouth. In Lotte's case, it was pretty much the same, since her parents had moved into her house after the accident to help her. So, in truth, a thing like that only made her feel less alone.

The apartment was tiny, but the living room gave Lotte a cozy vibe as soon as she entered it. The furnishing and decorations were, like Kenley's way of dressing, a mix between comfort and style. The walls were white, the curtains too, and the lamps had a simple design. But the place had a few colorful touches, like a big blue sofa with yellow pillows, a green- and timber-colored armchair and a cute little pastel pink vase.

"Do you want to sit down on the sofa? Can I bring you anything? Do you want anything to drink?" His hospitality was too precious for her world.

"I would appreciate some help getting out of this ... *thing*, thank you." Lotte had managed to move herself from her wheelchair and the sofa at her house a handful of times, but she hadn't mastered it completely. Kenley's sofa was also a bit higher off the ground than hers, so as usual she preferred not to even try, thinking she would fail if she did so.

She put her arms around his neck. He managed to lift her up bridal style, despite not being one of those guys who spent hours at the gym, and put her down gently on the sofa next to them. Then Kenley sank down beside her. His body might have been strumming with energy, but his mind was worn out. It had been a fun, but exhausting evening for them both.

He faced her direction and said, "I'm happy you decided to give our little support group a try, otherwise Nova, Ian, Bernie and I never would have met you."

She couldn't stop herself from laughing about it as the memory replayed in her mind. "I thought I messed it up the first day ..."

"Don't worry about that! You can't really see that I'm blind." Kenley tried to act like everything was fine by giving her a comforting smile, but the way he dug his nails into the palm of his hand showed her the opposite.

Lotte put her elbow against the back of the sofa and rested her head against her hand. "It seems like you've adapted to this new life kind of quickly?"

They were suddenly a few inches closer to each other.

He sighed. "I've just had to accept that ... this is my life now."

After a moment of silence, she asked with a slightly concerned tone, "Is there a way for you to get your sight back?"

Kenley furrowed his eyebrows and tilted his head down, probably in an attempt to hide his facial expression. "I don't want to keep my hopes up, you know? It could come back by itself, but I honestly doubt it at this point. I think surgery is *it*."

He would love to be able to see again, but lately he'd learned to appreciate the *little things* in life, knowing very well that going through surgery, and potentially gaining his sight back, wasn't equivalent to success. He was also aware there were many people in the world who had it way worse than him. He shouldn't complain, he had his cane, glasses that protected his eyes and also helpful people around him. What else could he ask for?

Sometimes though, he thought about whether his life would look any different if he had driven away only a minute earlier, or later. Or how different he would feel in his heart, knowing he'd never said certain things to the person who had once been very special to him. But what was done was done. Slowly he was adjusting to his new way of living. It had been tough and he'd shed many tears on the way, but he was getting the hang of it.

In the beginning, Lotte denied the fact that she needed a wheelchair, she wanted to believe her legs were temporarily hurt. When she started to come to terms with her new reality, the only thing she wanted to do was to stay at home, which her family got tired of quickly. She didn't have any goals and the future that she had planned for herself got erased. Lotte had thought about what her life would look like if she'd never made that one risky turn—also what her life would look like if she was ever able to walk again. But Kenley was right—they were alive and breathing.

"You know, Lotte, we can't change the past, but we can change our mindset for the future." He searched for her hand and placed his own on top of hers. "I'm here for you, you can always talk to me. I'm not leaving you unless you tell me to."

It was at this moment Lotte realized she might have been enjoying his company a bit too much. But she didn't know whether it was because she didn't have that many friends left, or because some sort of connection was actually beginning to form between them. She thought that maybe she'd imagined things. They hadn't known each other for long, after all.

"So, let's talk about something less ... deep. Do you have any hobbies? Something you like to do?" Kenley asked, trying to lighten up the mood a bit.

"I like to bake and read books. I think." Right after she said it, she realized how dumb it sounded. She was so unsure of herself these days. "What about you?"

"I love to draw."

"But you can't see?"

"Eh, that's kind of the charm of it."

While waiting for Lotte's dad to pick her up, they continued to talk, to get to know each other better. For a moment it was like no accidents had happened. Like her wheelchair and his cane didn't exist.

CHAPTER FIVE

Lotte had been on her phone, scrolling through the latest posts in her feed, when she noticed Kenley sitting on the other end of the sofa, making careful strokes on a piece of paper in front of him. "What are you drawing?" she asked.

Kenley quickly turned the paper toward him. "Oh eh, I'm just sketching a bit, just doodles, nothing special."

"Can I see?"

"Trust me, it … looks like a mess." He chuckled as he put what he held in his hands away. "But I can show you some of my drawings next time."

Well, she didn't mind that there was going to be a next time.

Suddenly Lotte's phone vibrated and lit up a spot in the darkening room. "Looks like my dad's here."

Kenley stood up. "Do you need help to—"

"Let me try it myself this time!" she cut in.

Kenley nodded as Lotte dragged her wheelchair closer to her. From the corner of her eye she could see him getting ready to catch her if anything would happen. In case he wouldn't be able to react in time, he put his hand on the side of the wheelchair, and knowing that he was there gave her some more confidence.

After Lotte managed to move from the sofa to her wheelchair without any problem, she began making her way toward the door. Kenley quickly put the sketch he made of her—at least, what he imagined she looked like, based on the few things he could glimpse—aside.

Kenley would later think back to this night as the moment he knew that he wouldn't be able to stand knowing she was unhappy. Lotte had so much more to give to the world. He wanted to make her understand that her life wasn't at all over just because she couldn't race or walk any longer. The hard task was to prove it in some way. It could take a while, but he was in for the challenge, in hope to show her it was possible to find joy outside of racing.

No matter how hard he tried, he found it impossible to draw a smile on the Lotte in his sketch.

Lotte's neighbors and the people living on her street were used to the sight of her in her wheelchair. But as soon as she went anywhere else, she could feel eyes piercing her back and heads turning in her direction, like they had never seen a wheelchair before. She always tried not to make eye contact with those people. If she did, she was met with awkward looks. It was hard to avoid all the whispering though. Some knew who she was and tried to take photos of her when they thought she wouldn't notice —which was another reason why she preferred to stay inside her house. Sure, people probably didn't mean to come off as rude, but Lotte's past experiences made her think the worst.

Down the street, Lotte's dad came walking toward them, shouting, *"Min skat!"* which was the nickname he used for all his loved ones.

She rolled her eyes. Could he *be* any louder? They didn't need more eyes on them.

"What? I'm trying to act normal, like you told me to!" he shouted right after, catching his daughter rolling her eyes at him from a distance.

As her dad greeted Kenley, Lotte could feel herself stop blinking; it was like she was afraid her dad would mess things up by telling Kenley embarrassing stories—like he had managed to do on several occasions in the past, sometimes purposely, and sometimes without even knowing.

But to her surprise it went smoothly. Her dad didn't tell Lotte there and then, but he liked Kenley's vibe—or maybe he was caught off guard by how different he was from what he'd expected. Kenley's arms weren't covered in massive sleeve tattoos, he didn't wear that typical bad boy leather jacket and he didn't reek of cigarette-smoke, like the other guys he'd had to deal with before. Kenley was refreshingly quite the opposite.

As they said their goodbyes, Kenley turned around to head toward his apartment. Her dad grinned at her and whispered, "I approve!"

Lotte tried her best to explain that she barely knew the guy. But she failed miserably at convincing her dad of the many reasons why she wasn't interested in Kenley at all. She soon realized it wasn't worth it and that no one would believe her lies. No matter what she said, her dad would joke about it and refer to Kenley as her "boyfriend" for the rest of the week.

Not everyone in the family was as sold on the idea though. Right after Lotte woke up the next day her mom, as usual, asked too many questions; it was like she had committed a crime and was getting taken through an interrogation.

"So, you met this guy at therapy? Why is he there?" her mom asked, with a very judgmental tone as she crossed her arms over her chest.

"He's blind. Or well, not completely blind, but …" Lotte muttered, before her mom began to give Lotte one of her long life lessons on why her daughter's situation was already complicated enough and how she could barely take care of herself. Hanging out with a blind guy was probably not the best idea, according to her. Ironic coming from the woman who'd wanted her daughter to leave the house and start socializing again.

The past couple of years Lotte had brought many guys home to meet her parents, but none of those relationships had lasted long, nor had they ended on a good note. Like her forty-eight hour relationship with a top-ranked tennis player or her impromptu—and quickly annulled—Vegas marriage to a well-known singer, who'd written at least five songs about her—all hits. Along with all her other romances that had somehow made headlines one after the other because, apparently, they were a source of entertainment.

With that in mind, she understood why her mom reacted the way she did, even though Lotte never once hinted she was interested in Kenley. The Lotte from before the crash was different from the Lotte of today. Back then, she used to fall in and out of love very easily.

Before her mom left Lotte's room she turned around to say that she thought it was great Lotte had found a *friend* to talk to, as she tried to give her daughter a slight smile, her empty gaze saying the opposite.

Lotte was alone. Most of her former friendships turned out to be all about fame and money. They only reminded her of what she couldn't have and couldn't do. It wasn't worth thinking about. She was disappointed in herself that it took a crash to realize that she would be much better off without them; how had she not seen how fake they were? After the crash, Lotte realized she was like a shadow in the group, despite having always walked first in line. They cared about who she'd become—one of the best racers in the world. Not *her*. Most of them hadn't even cared to contact her since she lost her title.

That night with Kenley at the amusement park, she felt important and seen in a more authentic way than when she was overwhelmed with cameras, prizes and champagne. It was a feeling she never wanted to let go of. She knew that he'd probably only done it to be friendly, but he was genuine and she wouldn't mind keeping someone like him close. Lotte believed he was a good one, even without knowing what he was hiding under his shell.

* * *

The weather that morning was pleasant; the sky was clear, it was sunny and the temperature was mild, which made Lotte decide to eat her breakfast outside on her porch. She broke a pattern yesterday by having a late night out, so why not continue to change some habits while she was at it?

One day at a time, brick by brick.

She had ten calm minutes before she heard sounds from the kitchen. Her parents were out in the garden, working and cleaning; it obviously couldn't be them. She heard more sounds. Just as she was about to turn around and take a peek at what was happening, her sister stormed out on the porch, with her breakfast in her hands—something Lotte definitely didn't expect. She thought Lykke was in another city, studying and having fun with her friends. Probably, since she'd taken to ignoring her sister's calls, she completely missed the fact that she had planned to visit.

"Why have you been ignoring me?" Lykke asked bluntly, right before she took a bite of her sandwich and sat down at the table.

Lotte could do nothing else but stutter when her sister showed up after weeks of not seeing her, and asked her a question she had no good answer to. Lotte tilted her head; she couldn't look her sister in the eyes, not after all the previous excuses she'd used to make her stay away.

She quickly glanced up at her sister. "What are you doing here?"

"I'm checking up on you. I didn't know that was illegal," Lykke said, giving her a frustrated look as she put down the sandwich on a plate and took a sip of her tea instead.

Lotte could feel her knuckles almost turn white as she grabbed the fabric of her sweater. "You know these past months have been really tough."

"*That's* your excuse for ignoring me?" Lykke came with an instant reply; she didn't waste any time. She knew her sister would take the first opportunity to hide if she could.

"It's been hard, okay?" Lotte raised her voice and said, "After the accident, everyone looked at me with pity in their eyes. Even you!" Her chest burned with anger and she had to concentrate to prevent the many tears she had stored from bursting out.

Lykke put down her mug with a bang, "Jeez, it's called being worried!" She met Lotte's already empty gaze and continued, "Those ghosts inside your head don't only affect you."

Lotte had tried to not think too much of Lykke. They used to be really close, they used to tell each other everything, but not anymore. Lykke had become like one of those friends she called a couple of times a year. Lotte didn't want it to be that way, but she was done with always being pitied upon when she visited. She knew she was a big part of the problem, she knew she was hard to read and hard to understand, but she couldn't help it. Some days she wanted people to feel bad for her, some days she wanted everyone to pretend the crash had never happened, and some days she was incredibly envious of the things she didn't have, like functioning legs and a bright future full of possibilities—something Lykke had.

Her whole life, Lykke had moved from city to city because of Lotte, because of her career, her racing. She'd never had much of a choice, until she was old enough to go to college. Everything had always been about Lotte.

Lykke was used to living in the shadow of her successful sister, but she'd always supported her, since she knew how much racing meant to Lotte and the whole family. But when Lykke needed Lotte the most, she wasn't there for her. It was like she was erased from earth. Despite the fact that she sometimes called Lotte ten times a day and left messages, she never replied, which left Lykke with clouded thoughts herself. Lykke still checked with their parents from time to time to get an update on how her sister was doing, but she knew that they sugar-coated things to keep her from becoming too worried.

With a yearning look on her face, Lykke said, "I just want my sister back."

As Lotte saw Lykke's eyes tearing up, a sinking feeling filled her chest. When parting her lips, the only thing that came out was a shaky, "I'm sorry." She knew it wasn't enough to heal all the wounds, but at least it was something.

One day at a time, brick by brick.

Lykke sighed and looked over at their parents, who had now begun deep cleaning the small greenhouse at the other end of the garden. She had expected a better apology after everything. Lykke felt just like the flowers and plants their parents threw in the container—wilted and colorless.

"I guess mom and dad knew you were coming?" Lotte asked.

Before standing up, Lykke grabbed her sandwich and took another bite. "They replied to my messages, so yes, they knew," she sighed, as she adjusted her shirt that had a smiling rain cloud on it, and began walking down the steps of the porch. "Are you coming?"

Lotte went after her, but instead of using the steps, she used the ramp her parents had built for her.

***

The sky started to resemble a color palette as the sun was on its way down. Back inside, Lotte saw her chance to rest a bit. After being out in the garden most of the day, she could feel her eyelids becoming heavier, and her upper body sore after sitting for too long in a slumped position.

The couch in front of her seemed to be the loveliest thing in the world at that moment.

But as usual when the clock showed it was close to dinner time, her dad turned the speaker on to the highest volume possible, blasting some Danish bangers. So much for some peace and quiet. She grabbed a pillow and put it over her head, trying to shut the music out, but it was impossible with her dad now singing along to the songs playing. The kitchen was in the center of the house, making each tune spread like wildfire—you couldn't escape from it even if you tried.

Lotte's mom attempted to sneak behind her husband to grab a glass of wine before dinner, but she didn't even have time to grab hold of the bottle before the crazy man who was dancing in the kitchen grabbed her by her waist, spinning her around like the ballerina she'd once been. It was hopeless to even try to fall into a slumber, with the laughter echoing through the whole residence.

Although it bothered Lotte, since she wanted to take a nap so badly, she adored her parents, regardless of their silly dances and ideas. Her parents had loved each other for twenty-five summers and it seemed like they loved each other more and more as the years passed by. They had a rocky start to their relationship and they had made people disappointed on the way, but they always had each other, through thick and thin.

Her dad always referred to his daughters as the "greatest mistakes of his life," as a joke. Lotte was born when her parents were twenty-one. A lot of people doubted them and their ability to take care of a kid and then not long after, two. They had all odds stacked against them, yet they still danced around the kitchen two and a half decades later. The infinite love they had for each other was something Lotte wanted to feel one day too.

She loved how they loved each other.

"Hva' så?" Lykke walked up behind her sister to ask what she was up to.

Lost in her own little bubble, the question startled Lotte.

Lykke leaned against the couch and said, "Aren't they adorable?"

"Indeed, they are." Lotte kept her eyes locked in the same direction. "They act like they are our age sometimes though."

"Can we blame them? We took their best years away from them!" Lykke shook her head and laughed, then she glanced at her sister with a playful look on her face. "Maybe we should join them?"

"Well, I can't, obviously," she replied, sounding more disappointed than she intended. "But I would love to see you join their little party over there." She faked a smile to show Lykke her approval.

When Lotte was a teen, she found things like those dance parties really embarrassing. She used to walk past the kitchen and pretend like it wasn't happening, shutting the door to her room.

Now, when her legs weren't working as they should, she would do anything to be able to dance like crazy in the kitchen. Seeing them having so much fun made her want to experience it too.

Suddenly, she noticed her dad walking toward her right before the song hit its chorus. He lifted her up from the sofa and into his arms. Then he started to hop and dance around with her as all four family members sang along to songs the sisters had listened to since they were kids. It didn't take long until she was lost in the moment too.

Her family was definitely weird—in a good way. She loved them more than anything else, although it wasn't often she expressed it. Lotte wasn't the best when it came to actually telling people how she felt; how much she loved and appreciated them. But she hoped each of them knew how much they meant to her.

She didn't want the moment to end, but they all stopped dancing when Lotte's phone rang a few meters away from them. It was hard to hear it at first, due to the music, but it buzzed several times and as the tune finally ended, it started up again. Lykke walked up to the sofa and grabbed Lotte's phone, since it seemed like it was urgent after several notifications.

"Here you go," Lykke said as she handed over the phone to her sister.

Her dad put Lotte down on a chair at the kitchen table as she looked at the phone screen, which showed a number she didn't recognize. Despite that, she pressed on the green symbol and brought the phone to her ear.

On the other end was Fajah, whose voice turned into a low murmur because of the wind whistling by where she was. "Hi hun, I hope I'm not interrupting you in the middle of dinner or anything, but do you have a minute?"

"Oh, yes of course, how can I help?" Lotte answered, glancing at her family standing a few meters away.

What must have been Fajah's heels made a loud echoing sound as she walked up a stairwell. A hint of worry came through the line as she asked, "Have you possibly heard from Kenley?"

"No I haven't. Why?"

"I've looked everywhere, and tried to call him, but he's not picking up." She took a deep breath, trying to calm herself down before she continued, "I can't find him."

CHAPTER SIX

Lykke pulled out a chair from the kitchen table and sat down in front of Lotte. "What was that about?" she asked.

Looking down at her phone screen, Lotte answered: "It's Kenley, you know that guy I—yeah ... apparently he tried to take a walk by himself, but he couldn't find his way home. I helped his aunt track his phone and eventually she found him. Everything ... is fine."

"That guy from therapy you mentioned?" Lykke asked.

Lotte nodded. "Yeah, that's him." Her head and heart were still pounding as she imagined the scene in her mind. Him, completely alone, in an unknown place in the city as it got darker, not knowing where to go.

Lykke drew invisible circles on the table with her finger, debating if it was worth pressing about this whole Lotte-Kenley-situation. "So, why did his aunt call *you*?"

"I guess Fajah wanted to check if I had an idea where he could be?" She could see Lykke wasn't fully satisfied with that answer.

"Is he cute?" she asked, leaning forward.

Lotte could feel her cheeks turning red. "No, or well, yes, no, I mean—"

"Did you just blush?" Lykke's eyes widened. "Since dad has met your man, I want to meet him too!"

"He's not ... We're not ..." she trailed off. But before Lotte could finish the sentence, her sister put her hands over her own ears to show that she refused to hear any more of the nonsense that came out of Lotte's mouth. Lotte began to talk very loudly, to make sure her sister heard everything she said: "I'm not interested in him! I've literally hung out with him like ... *twice!?*"

"Oh, does that mean he's still on the market?" Lykke saw her chance to joke about the situation and teasing her sister was her specialty. "Dad spoke highly of him. Maybe I should shoot my shot then?"

"Stop it," Lotte grumbled.

Lykke winked at her sister. "Don't worry, I won't put my paws on your man!" She made some sort of gesture with her hands, showing her non-existent claws as she attempted to growl like a lion but ended up sounding like a purring kitten. Then she walked out of the room and left Lotte more embarrassed than ever.

The next day, Lotte had to set her alarm quite early. Nova had called all the group members to an additional meeting that week, to discuss plans for a trip she'd planned for them. Usually, Lotte didn't have a problem waking up before sunrise, but for the past few months she'd been sleeping in almost every day. She wasn't sold on Nova's idea either, since she hadn't properly left the house for a long time. It made her tempted to "accidentally" fall asleep again and then "accidentally" skip the meeting.

She was afraid to do things outside her comfort zone and that trip was something that triggered all the warning bells. But she was pretty sure Kenley was going to be at the meeting and she wanted more than anything to check up on him after the little incident the day before. Knowing that he would be there, was enough for Lotte to collect enough strength to make her way out of bed.

While sitting in the passenger seat in the car, she observed random people who were running late for work and people who, for whatever reason, preferred to go for a jog over sleeping. Across the road, Kenley stood with his cane, probably waiting for Nova to show up, since she usually helped him inside the massive building the support group's sessions were held in. To Kenley, women and men rushing from left and right inside the building were almost as dangerous as walking on the outside, close to the moving vehicles. Not many saw his cane and some pretended like he didn't exist when they saw him struggle.

As Lotte's dad dropped her off, she slowly made her way closer to Kenley. When she was only a few meters away, she nearly lifted her hand to wave at him, before she remembered it would be futile. "Hey, Kenley," she said in a faint whisper.

After looking around for a few seconds, Kenley turned his head to the right, facing her. "Oh, hi ..."

"How are you?" Lotte said brightly, trying to act like she hadn't been worried and thinking of him the whole night.

"Oh, I'm fine, I'm just too stubborn for my own good sometimes." He shook his head and grinned. "It sounds so silly that I got lost."

"I don't think it's silly." She hoped he believed she was being genuine. Lotte knew that feeling, guilt mixed with embarrassment, which she felt each time she had to call for someone to help her do something many people managed without any problem.

"Thank you for helping Fajah by the way."

Seeing Kenley's sad face made Lotte want to jump up from

her wheelchair and hug him, but she couldn't; once again feeling so limited. Instead she reached for his hand and gave it a squeeze, just like she did the night at the amusement park.

She wanted more than anything to embrace him.

A moment later, a whistle down the street made Lotte travel back to the present again, instead of diving deeper into the dark places of her mind.

"So what do you say?" Ian shouted. "This trip is going to be dope!"

Lotte tried her best to fake excitement by forcing a smile on her face, but she must have failed miserably.

"Yes Lotte, of course you're coming with us!" Ian exclaimed, as a broad smirk took over his face. "You're kind of stuck with us now."

Nova came up right behind him. "Oh, don't worry girl, you're safe with us!" She grabbed Kenley by the arm and started to pat with her hand on his bicep. "And worst-case scenario, Kenley is strong … *I think*. He can carry you!"

Hearing those words, Lotte could feel her cheeks turn into some sort of scarlet shade again. Luckily Kenley couldn't see it—that would have been way worse. But the awkward tension was still lingering in the air for a minute, so she stayed silent and fiddled with the charm on her necklace, trying not to add fuel to the fire.

"When is this trip?" Kenley wondered aloud.

Nova picked up her phone and checked her calendar to make sure. "We were planning on leaving in a few days, maybe?"

"We'll only be gone for a couple of days. It takes a few hours to get there though," Ian replied, trying his best to garner excitement about the trip. "Short and sweet, just the way I like it!"

Nova snorted.

Lotte clutched her hands in her lap, watching her knuckles slowly turn white. "Where are we going?"

Nova gave Lotte an unsure smile. She knew deep down that Lotte probably wouldn't be very fond of it. "Well, I hope you like snow?"

Kenley kneeled to make sure that his eyes were at about the same level as Lotte's. "Of course, if it doesn't feel right, no need to feel pressured to come with us." His words brought her some comfort. "We would just really enjoy your company," he said and smiled, making those tiny creases in his cheeks visible again.

How could she say no to that?

To the others' surprise, Lotte straightened her back and said, "Let me check if I can find other tires for my wheelchair at home."

Nova put her hands to her sides and let out the breath she'd been holding. "Phew, because we were running out of arguments to win you over!"

Right after, Ian held up his phone, winked at Lotte and said, "Perfect, because I just booked hotel rooms."

Kenley stood up and turned away from Lotte for a short moment, in an attempt to disguise the wide smile creeping across his face—but Lotte had already seen it.

The anxious feeling didn't disappear right away for her though. She could still feel her palms becoming sweaty at the mere thought of the trip. Traveling with her wheelchair was something she'd tried to avoid as much as possible. In her opinion, it made everything much harder, not only for herself, but to everyone around her too. But they were right. She had to loosen up a bit.

Ian and Kenley had begun walking toward the entrance of the building, leaving only Nova and Lotte outside, along with some passersby.

"Do you maybe want to hang out later?" Nova asked.

Lotte made a quick scan of her surroundings to make sure no one else stood there. "Me?"

"Yes, you!" Nova chuckled. "I was planning on going to the stables after the session, do you want to come with me?"

Lotte tucked a hair strand behind her ear and said, "Oh uh, sure!"

"I'm stoked to finally have a girl to talk to around here! I love the boys, but ... you know ... men," Nova said, shrugging.

A laugh escaped Lotte's lips. Then they headed toward the entrance too.

* * *

After a twenty-minute-long drive in Nova's yellow vintage Volkswagen Beetle, the landscape shifted from crowded streets and giant buildings to an idyllic landscape with massive golden fields and woodlands. They passed a few pastures. Just watching a bunch of sheep exist in harmony was extremely soothing for the soul; she could see why Nova had no problem staying there for entire days.

The stable building was small and compact, there was only room for about four to five horses in there. It was probably an old barn, since the walls and the ceiling were made out of timber and the only natural light in there came from the few windows together with the many gaps in the walls. As Nova walked further inside, she had to switch on a flickering lamp to be able to find the box with all the brushes in it.

After collecting everything she needed, she walked toward a cream-colored horse with a snow-white mane and started to brush it in slow and gentle movements.

Lotte admired Nova's horse from a couple of meters away. "He's so beautiful!"

"He's my pearl, that's for sure," Nova replied in a very proud motherly tone. But her bright smile was abruptly taken over by sorrow. "There's a reason why I wanted to bring you here today," she said, beginning to brush more intensely.

Nova saw Lotte's frown, so she added, "Sometimes the thing we love the most, can hurt us in ways we never imagined." Nova threw the brush back into the box and started to braid the horse's mane to have something else to focus on.

At a loss for words, Lotte sat completely still. She felt a lump in her throat start to form as Nova's words went on repeat in her mind: *The thing we love the most. The thing we love the most. The thing we love the most. Damage. Pain. Suffering.*

"It started out as an ordinary evening. As any other day, I was out riding my horse. We took the same paths, crossed the same acres." Nova's voice cracked. She took a deep breath, trying her best to remain calm. "Then suddenly, my horse heard a sound and bolted. I tried to make her stop, but she kept running. I don't remember much else from it other than the fact that she ran out on a road. Everything happened so … fast."

From the look on Nova's face, it seemed like she was reliving that fearful moment in her mind. With a blank stare, she tilted her head and watched her feet move some hay around on the ground. After gathering herself, she said, "I don't want to go into too much detail, but I think you can figure out the rest."

Nova put a bridle on the horse and led it onto the small hallway that went through the stables; the clip-clopping sounds from the hooves striking the pavement echoed around them.

Lotte looked up at Nova. "I'm happy to see that you've found your way back here."

"I've actually not sat on a horse for many years." Nova turned around and closed the gate behind her. "A few kids help me out with Rudolf here." She smiled slightly and began to pat Rudolf on his neck.

Nova kept thinking "maybe one day"; maybe one day she would be able to see the beauty of it again and not be afraid. But that would probably take a while. The horror she'd witnessed that evening, plus the mental and physical torment she went through, were hard to just forget. At first, she blamed the horse for all the scars she'd gotten on both the inside and the outside, but after a while she realized how stupid it seemed. Horses were animals, of course they tried to flee when scared. It was instinct.

Nova sighed. "It may look like I have a perfect life on the outside, but I'm fighting my own demons, just like Kenley and Ian." She grabbed Rudolf's halter and approached the door. "You're not alone, you're not weird for feeling the way you do."

"Thank you for sharing this with me. You're so brave."

Nova spun around and gave Lotte a knowing look. "And so are you."

They went outside the stables and Nova showed the way to her favorite spot, a place filled with a variety of late blooming pink and purple flowers, close to a lake. They stayed there for a couple of hours. They talked a lot, played a few card games, and ate a lot of sweets; they did a lot of things that kept Lotte in the present. And did she feel better not having racing on her mind for a whole day straight?

Definitely.

That afternoon when they hung out meant more to Lotte than Nova ever could have imagined. She finally felt like she belonged somewhere. Nova, Ian, Kenley and Bernie didn't look at her like she was some sort of mentally unstable alien. They took her seriously, since they all had been, or were in, a similar state of mind.

* * *

Later that same day in an apartment close to the city center, Kenley sat on the sofa, with a sketchbook in one hand and a pencil in the other. He had nothing else to do.

With Fajah's pen-marking-system, he grabbed what he

believed to be a pink pencil and started to paint tiny flowers and stars on the paper in front of him. Looked upon by someone else, they probably seemed terrible, but to Kenley it was a sign of a fresh start. He usually picked the darker colors, like blood red, navy blue, dim gray or jet black. But his thoughts had been much lighter lately and he could catch a glimpse of some light in his mind. That evening, the colors he linked to agony and exhaustion were replaced with a light pink sky, with a touch of purple and orange, some tiny flowers in different pastel shades and a bright skyline.

"What's on your mind?" Fajah had been standing in the doorway between the hallway and the living room observing her nephew.

"Nothing much, I'm just sketching a bit." Kenley leaned forward and put the sketchbook and all the pencils on the table in front of him, as Fajah sat down beside him on the sofa.

He thought to himself for a few seconds, before he dropped the question he'd been thinking about for a while: "This may sound weird, but what does Lotte look like?"

Fajah chuckled. "She's beautiful. She has long brown hair and lovely hazel eyes, which I swear look golden in the reflecting sun; her skin has a shade of desert sand and there's a little mole on her left cheek." Fajah sighed, questioning whether it was right of her to talk about Lotte in that way, because there was such a slim chance that he would be able to see her beauty himself. But she knew that he wanted to know. "She's one of those people who can wear a potato sack and still manage to look absolutely stunning."

Kenley sank into the sofa. "I wish I could see her."

"Maybe one day ..." Fajah tried to sound optimistic, but it was hard given the circumstances. However, she was used to that type of situation, so she could sense when it was time to change the subject.

"Did you and Lotte have fun the other day, by the way?" she asked, to brighten up the mood a bit.

"It was fun."

"Gosh, she truly saved me when I couldn't find you, Kenny. This old lady needs to learn all the new functions on her phone. That tracking thing is a really smart invention!"

Fajah knew exactly how to make Kenley fall into her bubble of joy. She swore she could see at least the beginnings of a timid smile on his face. But sadly, bubbles were easy to pop.

"It was *Lotta* you called?" Delilah had heard enough of their conversation and she wasn't too sold on the subject they were talking about, which was clear from her hostile glare and the way she almost spat out the words. "I know you talked about this girl and that you wanted to prove something—" she yelled. "What's going on between you two?"

Kenley and Fajah had no clue what to reply, because no matter what, Delilah would probably use whatever they said against them anyway.

Delilah shot her son a warning look. "Please don't tell me that my son is unfaithful!?"

"Don't go there mom …"

Fajah glared at her sister. "Delilah, that's enough!"

"Your life will be twice as hard, Kenny. I'm just looking out for you, please understand that!" Delilah begged, hoping to win Kenley over to her side.

Kenley clenched his fists. "I never said we're dating or anything!" He felt like a ticking bomb, ready to explode at any second. His mom, who used to be so loving and caring, had turned into a stranger he didn't want anything to do with. He couldn't have a proper conversation with her anymore. She always brought up Joanne in one way or another. Many times she didn't do it on purpose, but for some reason it always managed to slip off her tongue.

Kenley wasn't in the mood to have one of *those* chats. He walked down the hallway, past his mom, into his room and slammed the door shut with a bang behind him.

"You and I are having a talk in a few minutes, sister," Fajah said, not meeting Delilah's eyes, as she walked up to Kenley's door.

Left alone in the living room, Delilah leaned against the wall, setting her gaze on the window, looking at her own miserable reflection mixed with the night sky and dozens of tiny lights. She knew that the aftermath of Kenley's accident changed her; she was far from proud of it. But she had already done too much damage and no matter how much she tried, she always ended up making things worse. She was afraid that it had been too long, that her son would never be able to look at her the same way again.

Her sight was a bit foggy from the tears she tried to hold in, so when she put down her handbag on the coffee table in the living room, she accidentally spilled a glass of water off it. The drawing lying on the table, once filled with bright and joyful sketches, quickly became a bloodbath of colors as she watched the water drown every inch of it.

Lotte tried to give herself a pep talk as she planned how she was going to move herself from her wheelchair to one of the sofas in her house. She glanced at the transfer board leaning against the wall a few meters away, but chose to try without it. She had done it at Kenley's all by herself, so why shouldn't she be able to do it again? Lotte had also watched a lot of tutorials on how to transfer from a wheelchair to a sofa and she had practiced it with her parents. It had been a long time since she felt so confident, so she thought, *Why not make the best out of it?*

As she was about to reach the sofa, she lost her balance and slipped. She hit her head on the coffee table standing in front of it, falling to the floor.

Lotte was used to it, the false hope. Many times after the accident she thought things were starting to get better, but each time something got in the way and took her back to square one. When she finally found herself rising and when she could glimpse some happiness at the end of the horizon, something always made the darkness in her mind return, clouds covering her sky.

She wasn't alone in feeling that way. As she slowly lost consciousness from her fall, a blind man fell to his knees in despair.

CHAPTER SEVEN

It was a rainy and gloomy day in October and nothing was going well—at least not for Lotte. It wasn't that early in the morning, but the only light came from a lamp in a corner of her room. No sunbeams were able to fight their way through the curtains with the dark gray clouds covering the sky. It made it hard to get out of bed, especially since she wasn't used to setting the alarm clock. Nowadays she could wake up whenever she felt like it.

After minutes of hesitation she sat up on the edge of her king-size bed and looked down on her feet, wishing for a miracle overnight—but she could still not feel a thing. Her mom came into the room and helped her into the wheelchair, since she didn't want to do it all by herself after her mild concussion from the other day. On the way out of her room, she didn't even give the mirror a single glance. The new bruises in her collection made her feel even more like a failure. They stung and pulsated, but luckily it wasn't anything too serious.

Lotte sat in silence by the kitchen table that morning, eating her breakfast, when the doorbell rang. Her mom opened the door, but Lotte joined her just a moment later, after recognizing the familiar voices.

In the garden stood Kenley, Nova and Ian.

She'd once thought going to therapy would be another mistake to add to her long list of mishaps, but she was surprised at how much lighter her heart felt since she started going. At this point, they had mostly touched the surface, but Lotte had befriended new people, people she could call her friends—people she could rely on if she needed to.

Although they hadn't spent much time together, they cared about her much more than people who had known her for much longer. They weren't the kind of people who would go out partying and carrying on with their lives like nothing had happened, when someone they cared about was in the emergency room.

Ian put down a paper bag filled with donuts on the ground. "Since you can't come to the party, we brought the party to you!"

Lotte was in the middle of eating her breakfast, but a donut or two was never wrong, no matter what time of day it was.

All four hung out for a little while in the garden, until a few left, knowing Lotte had to rest, not to make the pounding in her head worse.

Ian gave Nova a drive home—leaving her and Kenley.

He followed Lotte back into her room and helped her up on her bed, before making himself comfortable in an armchair next to it.

"Do you want to tell me what happened?" he asked.

"It's silly ... really silly," Lotte mumbled.

"Don't forget about the time I got lost," Kenley said, inching closer, "It can't be sillier than that, right?"

Thinking back on what happened to her the other night, she sighed and buried her face in her hands. "I fell when I tried to move from my wheelchair to the sofa. I hit my head on a table ... and then the floor. But I-I'm fine, I just have bruises."

Kenley moved even closer, so close that he could reach her face with his hand. He traced his fingers over her skin, comforting her. She thought he would laugh at her, but of course he didn't. Kenley wasn't like other people she'd met. Instead, he caressed her cheek carefully with his hand as he felt the contours of her face: every edge, every bruise, and her scar. Lotte saw her chance to finally give him that hug she'd wanted to give him so badly two days earlier.

He stayed with her the whole day. Most of the time though, the only thing she did was lay down and rest. Truth was, he would actually rather spend time with her, doing nothing, than doing something with anyone else.

Kenley didn't leave her like others had in the past. When she was asleep, he continued to work on his sketches and when she was awake, he continued to keep her company and make her feel appreciated, at times touching her hand gently and listening to what was on her mind.

* * *

"I take back what I said." Lotte's mom crossed her arms over her chest and shook her head as she took a peek into the living room and saw Kenley say goodbye to Lotte. "He's much better than David."

Lotte's dad looked at his wife in confusion. "I thought his name was Derek?"

She shrugged her shoulders. "Dylan, then?"

"Oh! I remember," he exclaimed. "Douchebag!"

"Ah you're right, that's his name! How could I forget?" She would normally not approve of such a joke, but she couldn't agree more with her husband.

It was her third day of resting and Lotte felt a lot better. The headache was gone and the bruises had slowly started to change color. Kenley also decided to come back to her house that following day—something she treasured a lot.

The trip was postponed because of Lotte's fall; she told them they could leave without her, but each of them said they wouldn't mind waiting, so they rescheduled. They wouldn't leave for another two days, but she wanted to be prepared, so in between naps she made sure to pack her bags. It made the whole thing feel more doable.

Before leaving, Kenley put a blanket over Lotte as she slowly drifted back to sleep. Then he tried to find his way out of the maze of furniture with the help of his cane. Since he'd been at her house the day before, he remembered where most things were placed—so it went fine.

As he reached the hallway, Lotte's mom came walking around the corner. "Thank you for keeping her company," she said.

"I don't mind. I enjoy it," Kenley assured her, "And thank you again for the dinner and everything, Mrs—"

"Please call me Karla!"

"My name is Rasmus by the way!" Lotte's dad shouted from the kitchen. It came so out of the blue that Karla startled and almost jumped, making her yell something back to him in Danish.

Karla followed Kenley outside and waited there with him until Fajah came and picked him up. In the beginning, she'd been skeptical about letting Lotte travel without her or Rasmus, but she'd come to realize Lotte would be in good hands. They wanted her to regain her freedom and that trip was a step in the right direction, even though they'd likely keep their phones close day and night until she came home—just in case.

* * *

It was a long route ahead to get to the destination. They had to make a few stops on the way so at least three of them could stretch their legs and so the fourth could stretch her arms and back without hitting the roof of the car. After they had lunch, they bought some snacks to prepare for the hours they had left.

As Lotte and Kenley sat outside on a bench, waiting for Nova and Ian to finish their argument about whether sweet or sour candy was the best, a car rushed by on a nearby road not too far away—way over the speed limit. Kenley could feel Lotte flinch, sitting next to her. Instantly he tried to locate her hand and ask if she was okay.

The sound of the wheels screeching against the asphalt together with the remains of gravel lying on the road, made a twinge of discomfort run down her spine. She squeezed her eyes shut, like she was waiting to hear the car drift off with a crash—waiting to hear the windows break into shards and the car to turn into something that was hard to identify.

She'd been told about the potential triggers many times.
She knew it was common after experiencing trauma.
She couldn't hold back the emotions that took over her body.
She couldn't stop picturing everything in her mind.

She was gasping for air, breathing rapidly. Kenley whispered something in her ear, but she couldn't hear what he said; she only felt how his breath tickled against her. A moment later, the palm of his hand grazed over the back of hers and he moved his thumb slowly back and forth. It had a calming effect that was much better than words.

She'd been practicing breathing techniques.
The images slowly faded away.
She knew she wasn't alone.

An almost-smile could be seen dimly on her lips. When she saw Nova and Ian turn to walk toward her and Kenley, she wished deep down that they would continue to argue for a little while longer. Because when he heard their footsteps in the gravel and their voices getting louder, he let go of her hand and stood up, ready to head toward their car.

After hours traveling northbound, they finally reached their winter wonderland, where the air was always fresh and cool, no matter what time of year it was. The sun had started to set as they arrived, the pink and orange light covered the village, making it look like an edited photo complete with several filters. It didn't matter in which direction she looked. The landscape was filled with white, powdery blankets of late October snow as far as her eyes could see, with tiny snowflakes falling to the ground around them.

But based on Nova's suitcase, it looked like she planned on going somewhere tropical—like she'd arrived at the wrong destination. Right after they checked in at a hotel off the main road, she managed to convince everyone to change into swimwear, since there was a heated pool on the bottom floor that Nova wanted to try out.

After she finally picked a swimsuit from all the ones she'd brought with her, she and Lotte covered up with sweatpants and hoodies, since it wasn't *that* warm inside the hotel, before meeting up with the guys in the lobby.

"Me and Ian are just going to call Bernie quickly. Why don't the two of you go ahead of us to the spa?" Nova said, nodding at Lotte and Kenley.

"Can't you do that yourself?" Ian asked Nova. "I need as many minutes as I can get in that spa!"

Nova walked toward Ian, grabbed his arm, and led him away from Lotte and Kenley. "Come on now pretty boy, we'll join them in ten."

Kenley walked up behind Lotte and folded his cane. "Lead the way, *my eyes!*"

* * *

Lotte guided them down the hallway to the spa area, describing the way so Kenley could get into the pool. She had to admit, she was worried he would slip and fall. Without thinking, she held her breath until she knew he was safe and sound in the water. Lotte herself sat on the edge of the pool, with only the parts she couldn't feel in the water. It was much safer that way.

Walking further into the pool, Kenley made sure that he still could feel the tiles under his feet. When he felt the warm water reaching higher and higher, the only parts above the surface being his head and shoulders, he turned around and walked in the direction of Lotte's voice instead.

"Why don't you join me?" he asked.

"I can't," she replied firmly.

Kenley walked closer to the edge where she sat. "I can help you if you want?" Worried it might have come off the wrong way, he added, "Only if you're comfortable with it, of course."

Lotte used to be confident, she never had any problem with showing skin. But since the accident, it was hard for her to even look at herself in the mirror. All she saw was scars. Ugly scars. Ugly and broad scars on her legs and back. Ugly scars other people would be disgusted seeing. She was insecure about the way her body looked, considering it had received some drastic changes without her approval, post-crash. In her eyes, she was far from beautiful and time after time she thought, *Who would want me?*

Kenley leaned against the edge of the pool with his elbow and found her hand, giving it a squeeze. "Do you trust me?"

Shivering and sweating, all at once, she pondered for a moment before she said, "I do ... I do trust you."

Once he got the green light, he wrapped his arms tightly around her body. Feeling safe and secure, she let herself relax and melt into his, before placing her arms around his neck—not really knowing where else to put them.

Unexpectedly he asked, "What do you look like, Lotte?"

The bashful smile on her face disappeared, like she needed time to think about how to describe the skin she'd lived in for almost two and a half decades. Stumbling on her words, she said, "I have brown hair and hazel eyes ..."

To Kenley's surprise she didn't tell him much. She usually described everything beautifully, very detailed, but when it came to herself, she was terse, matter-of-fact. The reason was that she didn't feel like a million bucks, or like the "sexiest woman alive" as a magazine had once claimed she was.

"I'm sure you can tell me more?"

She couldn't. There were many parts she didn't like about herself.

"I know I can't see you, but I have a hard time believing that you're anything but beautiful. Don't let those voices inside your head win out."

It was hard. She cared too much about other people's opinions.

The gap between them couldn't have been more than a couple of inches, and when she realized it, her heart began to beat faster; she didn't know what to do or what to say. It stressed her even more knowing that he waited for a reply. Lotte had lost count on how many guys she had dated over the years, it wasn't like her to freeze up like this. It felt like the first time she'd ever been that close to someone. The warm and fuzzy feeling made it hard for her to form words.

She couldn't help admiring him. Everything about him was too good to be true. He was so pure, so genuine, so charming.

It was hard not to like him.

She used to be impulsive, which sometimes led to better, and sometimes to worse things. Both giving her that feeling she used to have when she raced. A person she once knew had told her not to let a great opportunity pass her by and to live every moment like it would be her last; it might have sounded like a cliché, but it had helped her a lot with her career earlier in life.

During those silent seconds, the only racing she could hear was from her heart. She swallowed deeply and asked, "Can I kiss you?"

CHAPTER EIGHT

Kenley tilted his head slightly upwards in Lotte's direction, whispering his approval close to her lips—and without hesitation she met him halfway.

His lips were soft and warm, everything she had imagined them to be. She felt ashamed, at first, to admit to herself that she'd envisioned the scenario in her head at least twice before then. The actual kiss truly didn't disappoint. It was infinitely better. She knew that she would compare any kisses she might receive in the future to the kiss she shared with Kenley that night. It brought peace and comfort to her soul, it would for sure have made her weak in her knees if she could feel them.

Kenley on the other hand was conflicted. He knew very well it was wrong to kiss her, yet he couldn't stop himself from getting lost in the moment; he didn't want it to end. He tried to convince himself that the kiss was only a product of the heat of the moment, or the sake of not feeling so lonely. But the smile on his face told Lotte otherwise and although he tried to deny it in his mind, it was hard not to get drawn into the warmth that surrounded her. It was impossible to make his heart slow down when having her so close and feeling her fingers run through his curls felt so right.

When you can relate to someone, it's easier to build up a strong relationship, and Lotte believed that was exactly what they had. They were two outcasts who were comfortable around each other. To Kenley, it felt like she was the kind of person who came into your life when you least expected it, but needed it most.

Lotte liked the fact that Kenley could only judge her by her personality and not her looks. She wanted Kenley to be able to see again, but deep inside it worried her. What if the way she looked disappointed him? She wished she could see the version he had of her inside his mind.

Before the crash, she wore daring outfits and she used to put on layers of make-up to cover up the few insecurities she had. But no amount of make-up in the world would be able to cover up her horrendous scars and the less-than-flattering marks on her skin. Her wheelchair didn't really make her feel good about herself either. Kenley had done nothing but support her and make her feel better about herself. She wanted to believe everything he said, but he was blind after all.

As the sound of footsteps approached, and the noise of people talking got louder, Lotte and Kenley shared one last kiss before he helped her back to the poolside so she could grab a towel. She put the towel quickly over her legs, to hide the worst of her scars, as Nova and Ian came walking around the corner.

The kisses she and Kenley had shared—it was like they'd never happened. It was like they were hidden beneath the surface.

In the pool, Ian got a few minutes of peace with his face mask before Nova started to tease him for it and splashed water on him. All four of them, mostly Nova and Ian, continued to fool around in the water for another thirty minutes. But as the clock struck ten, they all parted ways and went to their rooms.

A blissful feeling would linger in Lotte until she fell asleep that night. She only wished the moment would have lasted longer. Kenley, on the other hand, would stay awake the whole night, wishing the kisses had never happened, regretting every second of it.

* * *

"So, what did you and Kenley do before we joined you last night?" Nova walked around in their hotel room, searching through her suitcase and her bag, trying to put together an outfit for the day.

Lotte looked out of the window, trying to appear mesmerized by all the tiny snowflakes falling peacefully to the ground, as she struggled to hide a smile. "Nothing much. We were just chatting."

"Sorry it took us a while to join you. Bernie *likes* to talk and Ian *loves* to talk." Nova laughed, before she added, "It was a never-ending phone call." She threw herself head first on her bed and grunted loudly.

Lotte put on her jacket and grabbed her gloves. Nova had told her they would spend most of the day outside, in the cold wintery wonderland. She hadn't shared many details though. Nova knew Lotte was rather pessimistic and wouldn't be the biggest fan of her ideas.

They met up with the guys in the lobby like the day before, but this time Lotte noticed Kenley's eyes were bloodshot, like he hadn't slept a wink. He didn't engage in any conversation at first either, instead he set his gaze on the floor, as though to make himself invisible. He had a steady grip around his cane with his right hand and with his left hand he dug his nails into the palm of his hand. It looked painful. It was something Lotte noticed him doing absentmindedly many times.

"Yesterday I saw that there's a part of the road outside the hotel that isn't properly shoveled. Kenley, maybe you can help Lotte if she needs it?" Nova asked.

For the first time in minutes he looked up from the floor. "I don't think I can, my arm hurts."

Ian gave Nova an anxious look, communicating through their eyes, like she could understand exactly what Ian tried to say, without him actually having to say it. "Ian then?" Nova tried not to make the situation more awkward than it was by changing the subject abruptly.

Ian nodded and left the hotel with Lotte, whose morning no longer gave her a reason to smile. Even though Kenley couldn't see her, it was clear he was trying to avoid facing her. Lotte was worried she'd messed it all up. If she could turn back time, she would make it so she never kissed him. The look on his face said it all—how much he regretted it, how much he didn't want to be near her.

Sadly, bubbles of joy are easy to pop.

They went to a small café in a nearby village to have brunch. By then, Kenley also started to warm up a bit to the group again. He took part in conversations and laughed—except for when Lotte was talking. He showed no interest in what she was saying and simply acted like she wasn't at the table. Lotte swallowed hard. She did everything in her power to fight back the tears. She had kissed many guys in her life, mostly when she was either drunk, high on adrenaline, or for other reasons she couldn't remember.

All meaningless kisses.

Seeing Kenley acting ignorant threw her off guard, because he'd been different with her. She wished he would have told her how he felt about the kiss right afterward, or at least given her a hint that it was too much, or too soon. Acting this way was probably his way of telling Lotte to keep her distance. Either way, her heart felt tortured, like someone had stomped on it.

Both Nova and Ian could see Lotte's teary eyes and hear the way she stumbled over her words. They understood that something was wrong, picking up on the pair's odd behavior.

As soon as they were back outside the café and stood in what had turned into a heavy snowfall, Nova grabbed hold of Kenley's arm. "Can I talk to you for a second?"

He followed Nova, wary of what would come. Together they walked out of sight from Lotte and Ian to a bus shelter where they sat down on the bench to shield themselves from the falling snow.

"What's up? You've been acting weird all morning," Nova said.

Kenley faced the ground and shook his head. "I messed up big time."

Nova started to run through all the events from the day before, in order to figure out when exactly something might have gone wrong.

Guilt was written all over Kenley's face as he said, "We kissed."

"You two kissed!?" Nova jumped up from the bench with excitement, but was taken aback as she examined his facial expression. "Wait. Rewind. What happened?"

Kenley let out a deep sigh and put his palm against his forehead. "I haven't told her about Joanne."

"Well, shit!" Nova didn't know what to say at first, she was stunned. "You kind of have to tell her now, because this isn't fair." She started to pace back and forth inside the tiny bus shelter, feeling her stress levels building up inside.

"It was just in the heat of the moment. I regret it, she probably—"

"Don't," Nova snorted. "I saw the look on her face." She stopped the pacing in front of him. "I know it's hard to talk about, but you have to tell her."

Kenley looked like he would much rather sink into the ground beneath them, than have to talk to Lotte again. But he had to come clean, and therefore Nova had to come up with a plan.

* * *

Ian walked next to Lotte along one of the paved and shoveled roads in the village, back to the hotel. He tried his best to make Lotte feel better about the situation and he continued to apologize on Kenley's behalf. "He ... has bad days sometimes. I guess today might be one of those days," Ian stated.

Lotte couldn't do much else other than nod, unable to get a word out.

"He's been through a lot and still is. His situation is a bit more complicated than mine. I can't even imagine what he's going through," he said, clenching his jaw.

Lotte looked up at Ian, wondering what he referred to.

He stopped walking, like he needed a few extra seconds to collect his thoughts. His eyes darted toward her as he said, "I'm not sure if anyone has mentioned it yet, but I had cancer."

It was like the air around was becoming colder by the second. All her muscles froze. She stuttered, no words would be enough to express what she felt. "I ... I ..."

Ian released a quick laugh. "I've been free from it for quite a while now, actually." He tried to form some sort of smile on his lips, but it was impossible for him to hide the worry he still felt. "It was just very hard for me and everyone around me, mentally."

Lotte could see, and hear, that it was hard for Ian to open up about it. The guy who was always full of energy, looked like he needed to find somewhere to charge his battery.

Ian inhaled some of the ice cold, but fresh, morning air as he continued, "I still remember my brother looking at me like I had already died. That kind of killed me on the inside."

Suddenly Lotte's problems seemed less important. On the one

hand, she had no idea she'd have that accident back in May, but on the other, she knew the risks that came with racing. In Ian's case, the blood inside his own body had started to kill him slowly. It happened without warning, it was something he couldn't prevent in any way.

Ian knew he was one of the lucky few. He'd been told he only had a few months left to live, but more than a year later he didn't have any symptoms left and felt healthier than ever before, at least physically. His mental state, though, could have certainly been stronger. Ian lived in constant fear that the cancer would come back; he lived in constant fear that he would have to go through everything—again. The long stays at the hospital, the chemo, the terror in everyone's eyes.

Lotte reached out her arms toward him and he followed up with a hug. Snow whirled around them and cool air caressed their cheeks, but neither of them felt the cold. The warmth they received from each other was more than enough to keep it away.

"You're so strong," she whispered, when she was level with his ear.

The snowfall calmed down after a little while and like in the morning, the dusting of snowflakes returned. Lotte, however, was still troubled, like she had a snowstorm inside of her.

It was an overwhelming day.

The four of them met up at the hotel a bit later. Nova stepped closer to Ian as soon as she came inside the door and whispered, "What do you do when you want two horses to get together?"

Ian gave Nova a puzzled look since her question came so unexpectedly.

"You put them in the same stable, alone!" She grabbed his hand and dragged him with her and left Lotte and Kenley alone in the hotel's lounge area, in the hope that they would settle the matter.

The radio was playing peaceful and relaxing music, but no music in the world would be able to calm Lotte's nerves. It had been a long time since she experienced being in such a tricky situation. They had barely said a word to each other the whole morning and now Kenley was stuck with her against his will.

"So, how has the trip been for you this far?" he asked.

She gave him a glare she wished he could see. "Are you kidding me right now? We kissed and now you're acting like you don't want to be near me!" The fire inside of her would be enough to burn down the whole building if she let it loose. There was a reason many called her "the Devil" after all.

Some things never change.

Kenley felt relieved he couldn't see her eyes as he sensed her tears building up—that would make him feel even worse about his actions. "I just wish it had been under different circumstances," he mumbled.

To Lotte, she felt like a clown tripping over its own feet, foolish. What could he possibly mean? The setting, the timing and the feelings—it was everything she could have wished for.

He was silent as he weighed his words carefully, before parting his lips and saying, "Lotte, I'm engaged."

CHAPTER NINE

Joanne was her name. She was in a coma.

Lotte wanted to be mad and maybe say something she would likely regret later, since Kenley had kept the truth from her. She'd assumed this girlfriend of his had died that day in the car crash. So many things had pointed to it. Kenley's actions, the effort and time he had spent with Lotte was something that strengthened her theory. But how could she let the flames loose, when it looked like his whole world was falling apart in front of her eyes?

Kenley and Joanne had gotten into a big fight right before the crash. He told her they'd already been "walking on thin ice." On top of that, he wasn't on the best terms with Joanne's family. They blamed him, even though a drunk driver had caused the head-on collision.

Kenley had been told the crash was his fault so many times that he'd started to believe it himself. After all, he'd been the one behind the steering wheel.

Maybe he could have done more to prevent it all from happening. Maybe he could have reacted quicker. Maybe, maybe, maybe.

"So, do you have any lovers you haven't told me about?"

Kenley asked between sobs. He tried to put on a brave face and joke about the things that bothered him as a coping mechanism. But it was hard when everything behind his shell started to show; it was clear he tried to move the focus to something else.

Lotte couldn't decide whether it made her heart lighter, or if it put more weight on her shoulders now that she knew the truth. Trying to form words, only stutters left her lips, as it felt like someone had knocked the air out of her lungs. "I-I've had a few," she answered. "I was in a relationship before the crash ... but it ended as soon as he saw my wheelchair." She shrugged her shoulders, attempting to make light of it, like it was no big deal, despite the fact that she could still feel her heart ache each time she thought about it.

"That just shows he clearly doesn't deserve you," Kenley stated, making the grim look return. "By the way, I'm planning on visiting Joanne at the hospital as soon as I get home. Do you want to come with me?" he asked, turning his head quickly in her direction as he rubbed the side of his neck with his hand.

Lotte was clearly feeling something for Kenley. Exactly what that was, she couldn't put her finger on. Going with him to the hospital sounded like a bad idea, especially since they were going to visit his fiancée. But he needed the support; it was something he lacked in his life.

They ended up talking for hours. They laughed together, they cried together and when they finally went outside again, the sky was almost pitch black. As Lotte looked above the crowns of the trees, she saw that the sky was covered in a curtain of blue and green. *Northern Lights.* They moved around in a peaceful rhythm in the night sky. It was a magical sight, something she'd never seen with her own eyes before.

Kenley was curious about what she was doing since she'd been silent for a minute. "What's on your mind?" he asked.

"Oh, sorry. I-I'm ... looking at the northern lights."

"What does it look like?" It was too dark outside; Kenley couldn't even catch a glimpse of it through his blurred vision.

He grasped the handles of her wheelchair and Lotte guided them down the road next to the hotel, which led to a field. He helped her out of her wheelchair and then they laid down on the snowy field and faced the sky; his arm clearly didn't hurt any longer since he had no problem lifting her.

It had stopped snowing, which made the sky incredibly clear and the lights so bright. Lotte described everything she saw in detail, making Kenley experience it too—or at least as much as possible. Like how it more or less looked like the lights were dancing, or running a marathon in the sky.

"What about the stars then? Can you see any?" he asked after a while.

Lotte put her hands behind her head and fixed her gaze on a constellation right above them. "I've never seen this many stars at once."

She found herself staring at the sky in wonder. She wanted more than anything to see a shooting star, not wanting to wait for the dandelions to bloom in her garden again to make a wish. There was light beyond the skyline that night and she wished for it to transfer over to her—but it never did. She was waiting for the next loss to come. She knew there was no use celebrating too soon.

Her smile faded as fast as it appeared.

During the third and last day of their trip, they explored the rest of the village they were staying in—mostly Lotte with Ian and Nova with Kenley.

But as night came, all four of them had no other choice but to work together, to be able to put up a tent in a clearing. Nova had kept the tent part a secret, since she knew two members of the group didn't like things too far outside of their comfort zones. Despite that, she decided to go with the idea anyway; she and Ian just wanted them to live a little.

"Are you sure we're not going to freeze to death? What if we all get hypothermia?" Kenley stood in front of Nova in the forest with several layers of clothes on and doubted his friend's choice of "hotel" for the night.

"If the sleeping bags and the blankets aren't enough," she said, before inhaling some of the cold evening air, making it look like fog left her mouth the moment she exhaled. "Body heat." Nova giggled and grabbed Kenley by the arm, before they made their way toward the tent.

Ian and Lotte chit-chatted a bit, curled up in their sleeping bags and blankets, while waiting for the others to join inside. Being on the verge of falling asleep, Lotte heard someone close the zipper of the tent for the night and felt Nova crawling over to her own spot, before laying down with her back against Lotte's, facing Ian.

The corners of Lotte's mouth curved upwards and relief washed over her as she felt Kenley lay down on her other side. When she opened her eyes, she didn't expect him to be facing her, but he was. She almost believed the dim light from the small lamp inside the tent made her eyes play tricks on her, or that it was a dream based on her wishful thinking, but he was right there, so close, only inches away.

Realizing it was wrong of her to feel that way killed off the bliss and wiped the hint of a smile off her face. It was better between them, but not good. For a few seconds she even wished she was at home, lying in her bed, alone, rolling her thumbs to the rhythm of the clock.

Almost like their minds aligned and he knew exactly what she was thinking, Kenley placed his hand over hers; it was one of the many innocent touches she'd received since she got to know the truth. They both wore many layers of clothing and their hands were covered by mittens, yet she still felt a shiver run through her.

* * *

The snowflakes falling from above gradually became raindrops splashing against the car on their way home. Kenley fell asleep only minutes after he sat down in the car and he kept his eyes closed for the rest of the drive. Lotte, on the other hand, stared out of the passenger window, looking at the scenery: trees, road signs, buildings—simply the things they passed on their way.

Ian and Nova dropped them off outside Kenley's apartment building, where Fajah stood waiting for them. Before they left for the hospital, Kenley put one foot inside the apartment and placed his and Lotte's bags on the floor. Lotte wondered to herself whether it was a good idea to go right after they arrived home from the trip, since they'd been sitting in a car for several hours. But as she thought about the information she had gathered so far —there were probably people he had to avoid. He couldn't choose the most comfortable hours.

Nurses directed them through several hallways inside the hospital. The more corridors they passed, the more Kenley's eyebrows furrowed, the corners of his mouth drawing down. Lotte couldn't decide what was most painful: the stinging, horrible and sadly familiar scent of soap and chemicals that lingered through every hallway of the hospital, or Kenley introducing himself as Joanne's fiancé to the doctor in front of them.

Kenley gave Lotte a gesture with his hand to show her it was okay to come with him. She had no idea what to expect, even though he'd tried to prepare her a bit in the car. Lotte was almost afraid to witness what was waiting for her inside those walls, so she moved slowly closer, peeking into the room.

It was a small room with light gray walls. The only colorful touches came from several "get-well-soon-cards," with different messages on them, standing on a tiny table. Next to the table was a bed, with wires attached to the person lying on it. Lotte went further into the room to be able to see what was hiding behind Kenley's back, but she became as still as a statue when she saw a woman, with porcelain pale skin and flaming red hair, looking lifeless just a few meters away.

Kenley squeezed Joanne's hand and cupped her cheek. Lotte saw the man she had become close to, looking at the woman he loved and probably never would stop loving. She had only been there for half a minute, but the sight was too much to handle. She felt incredibly guilty and empty on the inside, looking at a woman whose life had taken a turn way worse than hers, way too early. Joanne would most likely never be able to walk around the city, never be able to see the sky's breathtaking colors at dawn or dusk again. She thought about how she would feel if she were Joanne, and woke up, against all odds.

Replaced.

Lotte left the room and closed the door behind her gently, to make sure she didn't ruin Kenley's moment with Joanne even more. She knew she couldn't stay—staying was wrong in so many ways.

When she thought about it, she regretted agreeing to come with him in the first place, and she had no idea why Kenley chose to get as close to her as he did. Lotte doubted she could ever compare to Joanne, if she one day would wake up and therefore come back into the picture. Lotte didn't want to lose Kenley, but she knew that he belonged to someone else. It was better she left before she got any more attached.

Lotte was so overwhelmed with her own thoughts, that she

hadn't even realized Fajah had moved to sit beside her. "She's getting weaker and weaker each day that goes by," Fajah said. "I honestly don't think she has much time left."

Lotte fiddled with the charm on her necklace, dragged it back and forth across the golden chain. The corridor they were sitting in was completely silent; it was a difficult situation. She had to say something, or maybe Fajah expected her to say something? "How was she? I mean, Joanne," Lotte let slip.

"She was like the Energizer Bunny. She loved adventures, traveling, working out, singing and dancing," Fajah said, as she gave Lotte a strained smile. "She is a wonderful person, but to be honest, they don't have much in common. I feel horrible saying it, but their stars don't align, you know? There were too many lows the past year of their relationship. I'm pretty sure they managed to break up twice the week before the accident," she explained, before taking a loud sip of her coffee. "I think Kenley was in love with the thought of being in love."

Lotte sat completely still, silent, taking it all in. She felt as if the room was spinning around her.

Joanne.

He's engaged.

They were about to get married.

Fajah put her hand on Lotte's shoulder, looked straight into her eyes and said, "Kenley can't get over what he said that night."

Kenley and Joanne had argued a lot the week before the crash, but each time, they made up and everything turned out just fine. Until he said the things that would forever haunt his conscience. Wounds heal with time, but there was no cure to the pain his words had caused.

When they came back to his place, Kenley went to his room and lay down on his bed. He didn't even bother to change into something more comfortable; he was too mentally exhausted to care.

Lotte went to the bathroom to make sure her mascara wasn't smudged all over her face. It was hard to see from her angle since the mirror was placed higher up on the wall than she was used to, so she had to use her phone's front camera instead.

Moving between rooms was also a struggle she had every now and then; the thresholds in his apartment weren't that easy to pass. Kenley must have heard her struggle as she tried to enter his room, because he suddenly woke up from his nap and turned around to face her.

"Oh, sorry if I woke you up, I … I'm going home," she said.

Kenley yawned and sat up on the edge of his bed. "You're leaving?"

"I think you need some time alone."

"And if I don't want to be alone?"

Lotte gave him a serious look she knew he couldn't see. "I don't think that's a good idea. This is wrong." All the emotions she had held for herself that evening made her voice become shaky. "You're going to regret me, as much as you regretted the kiss." She wanted to believe she meant something to him—that she was something more than a distraction. "What do you even see in me?" Lotte almost shouted. "Oh wait, you can't actually see me!" she blurted out.

She didn't mean to say such a thing; she knew it was a sensitive subject. But the emotions took over—so much anger, so much sadness.

After a few seconds of complete silence, Kenley looked in Lotte's direction. "I don't need to see you to know you're amazing in every way possible." He sighed and shook his head before he hissed, "Why would I lie?"

"What if she wakes up? Now? For real? You're engaged!

How can you not understand how wrong this is?" Lotte gesticulated with her arms and hands to show her anger more clearly—which no one except for herself could see. But the venom in her voice alone was enough to make him wince.

Kenley raised his voice in a way Lotte had never heard before as he shouted, "I called her annoying and spoiled. I told her that I understood why she didn't have many friends left and why I disliked her!" He buried his face in his hands. "Those are a few of the last things I said to Joanne." He laid back down on the bed, letting the tears he'd been holding stream down his face.

Lotte put her hand on his ankle in a way to comfort him, since his chest and face were unreachable from where she sat. It was also at that very moment she saw a tiny tattoo on his foot. She tapped her finger on the little symbol which almost looked like a flower or a little plant with four leaves. With hesitation in her voice she asked, "What does this mean?"

"It's a Ghanaian Adinkra symbol, called Tabono. It represents strength, confidence and willpower to achieve dreams. Fajah has one too."

"When did you get it?"

Kenley chuckled through the tears as he remembered the story behind it. "When I turned eighteen, me and my badass aunt thought it was a good idea to go and get tattoos without mom knowing." He sighed, but this time he beamed in Lotte's direction with a twinkle in his eye.

A few minutes earlier, Lotte had been close to sending her parents a text message, asking if they could pick her up. But she deleted it. "Can you … help me up?" she asked.

She could glimpse those creases in his cheeks from where she sat, as he asked, "Weren't you supposed to leave?" He could imagine her rolling her eyes at him.

Sitting on the bed, they wrapped their arms around each other tightly, like they were afraid that if they ever let go, they would never meet each other again. Lotte snuggled up next to him; it was hard to not fall asleep in his embrace, which was surprising for someone who had something similar to insomnia.

Kenley was exploring her face with his hand, like it was a map: first her jaw and her cheekbone, then her nose, her lips and the tiny scar on her right cheek. He would have done anything to be able to see how angelic she looked when she fell into a slumber. But hearing her breathing slowly beside him was fine too.

Love wasn't a switch you could turn on and off, but it was possible for it to fade over time—that was exactly what had happened between Kenley and Joanne. The person she'd become before the crash wasn't the same person he'd once fallen in love with. Joanne would always have a special place in his heart, but she wasn't the one, even though he believed it at first. He just couldn't leave her when she was on the brink of never seeing the light of day again.

Kenley wasn't sure how to label his and Lotte's relationship, but he was positive she had come into his life for a reason. She gave him the will to live at a time he didn't have much to live for.

After a moment of thinking Lotte opened her eyes, leaned her elbow on the mattress beneath them and rested her head in the palm of her hand. "Since you can't see my scars ... maybe you want to feel them?" she asked, putting her hand on top of his.

Kenley lifted his head from the pillow, looked up at her and replied, "You sure?"

Lotte rolled up one of her sweatpant legs before grabbing hold of his hand and putting it right above her left knee, where one of the bigger scars was. It was long, broad and held a mixture of darker shades. She didn't even want to know what exactly might have caused such damage during the crash.

He slowly moved his hand along the scar. "Beautiful," the almost completely blind man stated, with his eyes closed.

"How do you know?"

"I just know."

Even though he could barely see anything, Lotte valued his words more than any person she'd met whose vision was intact.

"So, do you believe me?" he asked.

"More than I thought I would," she said.

"As you should."

Their faces were close to each other. It gave her a chance to admire his eyes, almost as dark as obsidian, once more. They always managed to hypnotize her, make her feel that fluttering feeling in her stomach and fill her with warmth. Looking into his eyes, she could see her future. She was just not sure how far into it she dared to glimpse.

He kept moving his hand along her scar. "You can't feel this, right?"

"No, I can't," she sighed.

He moved his hand further up, over the fabric of her sweatpants and rested his hand on her hip bone. "This?"

She made an effort with every cell in her body to feel something, but it was hard to tell whether the sensation she felt was actually his hand, or if it was her imagination deceiving her. "I'm not sure ..."

He proceeded to move it further up and stopped at her waist, which was partly bare from her cropped T-shirt. "This?"

"Yes, I can feel you now," she said, smiling, as she felt the warmth of his hand and his fingers moving like silk over her skin.

Kenley inched closer, which caused their noses to brush against each other before their lips met. She almost felt her toes curl—almost—especially when he began placing kisses down her neck and moving his hand along her upper body. She savored every second of it.

Having Kenley close and feeling him caressing her body, was something she wouldn't mind adding to her normal morning and night routine.

CHAPTER TEN

According to articles and posts Lotte had read online, sleeping next to someone you trust, or love, makes the oxytocin level in your body shoot almost through the roof. It makes your body feel relaxed, it makes you less anxious, it can help to ease pain and it can also lower your blood pressure—among other things. Of course, that doesn't mean everyone feels that way, but Lotte couldn't do anything but agree with those studies.

She had woken up twice that night, only to fall asleep again in a matter of seconds. Feeling his warm chest against her back, his breath against her neck, having his scent fill her nostrils and feeling him resting his arm around her like a protective barrier, made her feel secure—at least for the time being.

The dark curtains in his room made it look like it still was nighttime. It was only through the gap where the two curtains met, that sunbeams were able to shine through. Lotte sat up and stretched her arms before she turned around to face Kenley. He was still fast asleep and wrapped up in the duvet, like he had no plans of getting out of bed for at least two more hours.

Hygge.

She reached for her phone to check if she had received any new notifications. Lotte held her breath, thinking the worst, when she saw all the messages from Lykke. Then she realized her sister just wanted to make sure Lotte understood she had no choice but to spill all the tea the next time they saw each other. Apparently the fact that she stayed the night at Kenley's had reached the whole family at this point.

Putting the phone away and looking over at him, the corners of her mouth curled upward. She felt like a creep, watching him sleep, but it was hard not to when he was looking so peaceful and adorable, probably strolling around in some dream land. She moved around to lay on her belly and wrapped her arms around the pillow she rested her head on, which was where the feet were supposed to be.

After facing him for a few minutes she could see his lips form into a sleepy grin as he reached his arm out toward her, snuck it around her waist and pulled her closer. He moved his hand along her figure and let his fingers run down her spine, along her scar—all the parts she thought were unworthy.

An hour passed by until they were both out of bed and finally making their way toward the kitchen. Kenley lifted her up so she could sit against the wall on the counter top. She buttered her toast and took a bite, then she poured some chocolate milk into a small blue tea cup and took a sip, watching Kenley get his breakfast ready. Lotte found it impressive how well he managed to find everything he needed. He knew the bowls were in the cupboard closest to the fridge, he knew the spoons were in the second drawer from the top and that the strawberry yogurt was placed first in the bottom row of the refrigerator door. He had to remember where everything he used on a daily basis was placed and hoped that no one moved anything around. At times, when he made lunch or dinner, it happened that he grabbed the wrong ingredients from the cupboard.

"You've never thought of getting a dog?" Lotte asked in between taking bites of her toast.

"That would be really nice, but I have to spend my money on more important things." Kenley leaned his back against a counter in front of her and crossed his arms over his chest. "But I'm going to try to find a job soon. Fingers crossed I'll get one."

She tried to cheer him up by saying, "Oh, of course you will, it's hard not to like you."

"Not many companies want to hire a blind guy," he claimed.

Before the crash he'd been studying, in the hope of becoming a teacher one day. But after the crash he didn't have much motivation to keep doing so. Him being blind would make it easy to fall behind, since he wouldn't be able to read any of the material he received from the professors. He hadn't mastered braille yet either, which was another thing on his to-do list in the coming months, if his vision didn't improve.

Kenley walked toward Lotte and put his hands on the counter, caging her in. She'd lost count of how many times she told herself it was wrong to be that close to him since the previous night—yet she leaned in for a kiss. For once she felt happiness. Was it selfish of her to take someone else's place to be able to experience that?

"So, do you plan to look for a job?" Kenley asked, before planting a kiss on her forehead.

"I-I don't know. Maybe?" Lotte looked down at the cup she was holding in her hand. Even though he could barely see and definitely couldn't see her facial expression, she tried to avoid looking straight into his eyes; she could feel her cheeks burning. "I don't have a degree, which might be a problem." During the time when her racing career blossomed, people had asked her what she was going to do after the fun was over—for instance, if she planned on going to college. Was she going to find herself *a real job*? She'd laughed at their questions, telling them it was ridiculous. Racing was something she was going to do until her face ended up full of wrinkles.

"Fajah looks for new people to hire from time to time, to help her plan and organize stuff. I can always check with her?"

Lotte hadn't been told much about what Fajah did, any more than the fact that she owned her own fashion label in a building a few blocks from Delilah's apartment.

Lotte turned her head up again, put her cup aside, looked into his dreamy brown eyes and ran her fingers through his curls; it had become her new favorite thing. "You don't have to—"

"Can you start tomorrow?" Fajah came walking around the corner into the kitchen, with what looked like important documents in one hand and her coffee mug with the text "boss babe" on it in the other. Clearly she'd also stayed the night at Delilah's.

Lotte pushed Kenley an arm's length away as soon as she heard Fajah's voice, but her mischievous grin made Lotte believe she'd already seen, and heard, enough to understand what was going on. Still, Lotte looked like she'd seen a ghost and Kenley was trying, and failing, not to laugh.

Fajah leaned against the doorframe, pointed with her coffee mug in Kenley's direction and chuckled. "As Kenny said, I hire people sometimes to do stuff for me."

If Lotte's cheeks were rose red a minute earlier, they for sure had turned into scarlet now. She was sitting on a kitchen counter in an apartment belonging to the sister of her eventual new boss. Her hair was messy, she wore a shirt that definitely wasn't hers and a pair of old sweatpants. To fan the flames, she had slept in the same bed as said new boss' nephew the whole night.

Great. Perfect. Not awkward at all.

"Oh, uh, y-yeah, if you're sure?" Lotte's throat suddenly felt incredibly dry, like she'd had her mouth open all night. "What exactly do you want me to do?"

"Some easier administration work to begin with." Fajah filled her mug with more coffee, then she turned around, ready to head out. "Does that sound good? I can text you more details later today, I need to head to work."

"Sounds good. Thank you," Lotte mumbled as she tucked a strand of hair behind her ear, trying to tame the mess on her head a bit.

Fajah walked out to the hallway and as she was about to close the door behind her, she shouted, "You can continue on with whatever I interrupted now!" She closed the door and they could hear the sound of her heels, and her giggles, echoing through the stairwell.

"Seems like we have that solved then, eh?" Kenley put his bowl in the plate rack and threw the dish brush in the sink, then he walked toward Lotte again.

"That was ... unexpected." Lotte wrapped her arms around him, as he rested his head against her shoulder. He was still a bit sleepy, so he saw that as an opportunity to be able to drown in her embrace one more time.

"Don't worry too much about it, okay? Fajah likes you."

Hearing those last three words from Kenley caused a bit of hope to bloom inside of her. Nevertheless, it still felt like she was playing someone else's part, which quelled that blooming feeling inside of her and turned it to dust right away.

"So you are like the other woman!?" Lykke spit out the pasta from her mouth into a napkin in pure shock, realizing her sister's life had turned into one of those cliché movies she loved to watch.

"I wouldn't call myself that, but—"

"Yes, you are, Charlotte!"

"That's not even my name—"

"I know, but it sounds more serious!"

It was later in the afternoon and Lotte was back in her own home. Their dad had picked up Lykke from the train station a little after lunch. This time Lotte texted her sister first, and asked if she wanted to come over, which was out of the ordinary. Luckily, she had a day off from all the studying and was more than happy to meet up.

"What would you have done?" Lotte looked up at her sister, but Lykke's eyes weren't as reassuring as she'd hoped. "I'm in deep shit, aren't I?" Covering her face with her hands, she let out a dying-whale-sound. Joanne being in a coma truly made the situation much worse, since Kenley couldn't let her know that he wanted to end things between them for good.

"It's a weird situation you're in," Lykke said, her mouth full of food. "But if what he's telling you is true … then go for it!" Like it was an easy decision for Lotte to make, Lykke just shrugged her shoulders. "At least, that's what I'd do," she added.

"I feel bad … for Joanne," she whimpered. "I had a freaking make-out sesh with her fiancé yesterday!"

"When you put it like that, it actually sounds kind of bad …"

"You are not helping!"

"You literally told me—" Lykke grunted. "Okay never mind!" She sighed, pinching the bridge of her nose. "Not to be that person, but men like him don't fall from trees these days. I mean, if he really has fallen out of love with his fiancée …"

All Lykke wanted was for Lotte to find someone who valued her above everything. Because a guy who could continue a race and receive a trophy with a smile on his face, after seeing his girlfriend's car in pieces on the track, wasn't the one.

"I like Kenley. I like him a lot, actually," Lotte admitted. She had only known him for a little over two weeks, but they'd spent many long and meaningful days together. He was able to show his vulnerable side and in return, she shared the not so flattering parts about herself. "I finally feel some sort of happiness."

"I'm glad you have him in your life. But I wish it could be under different terms."

"Same. Right now it honestly feels like I'm borrowing him or something, to then later return him."

Lykke stood up and walked over to her sister and gave her a hug. "You'll always have me."

Lotte hugged her back. "I know. Same goes for you."

The sisters continued to catch up for a couple of more hours, just hanging out, like they used to do before the crash. She missed having Lykke around. She had missed her sense of humor, missed gossiping with her like they did in "the old days" and missed her confidence—especially her cool and colorful style that turned heads. Lykke brought her joy, and the best part was that she would never leave. That was important for Lotte to know, when she thought she might have to lose someone.

After spending the whole afternoon and evening with her family, her mind was a lot clearer. But later that night, when she went to her room to unpack all her bags, she was reminded of the trip—and of him. She wondered how he was coping with everything at that exact moment, if he was sad, anxious, scared, or if he needed someone.

Lotte wished he would have called her at least once that day, or even just sent her a voice message, so she could hear his voice before she went to bed. After spending the night at his place, her own bed, which used to feel warm and comfortable, suddenly felt too big—too cold and empty. She was on the verge of calling him, but she didn't want to come off as needy or annoying. After all, they weren't a couple or anything like that. Before she closed her eyes for the night she stayed up scrolling around on the internet for almost an hour, looking for service dogs for sale.

At the same time, in an apartment close to the city center, Kenley lay in his bed, listening to one of the audiobooks Lotte had recommended him. He hugged her pillow and sniffed the sweet fruity scent her perfume had left on it—wishing she was there.

CHAPTER ELEVEN

Lotte was supposed to meet Fajah in her office at nine o'clock in the morning. She woke up way earlier than she had to, making sure she was fully refreshed, in the hope of not accidentally saying anything stupid.

She looked through her wardrobe, trying to find something else other than sweaters and sweatpants to wear. In the back there was a pile of dresses she hadn't so much as glanced at in many months. She doubted they would look good on her now, or be comfortable to wear. She spotted a grayish dress, with some sort of ribbon-looking thing as a belt, in the bottom of the pile that was a bit looser and had a velvety soft fabric compared to the others. The dress was pretty, but she understood why her past self had put it in the bottom of the pile. It wasn't as curve-flattering and it wasn't a color bomb like the others; the grayish dress was something Lotte a year earlier would have thought was something a grandma would wear.

In the building where Fajah had her office, there were many people on their way to work. Some people walked across the lobby looking at their phones and some people were in such a hurry that they didn't think about the consequences of rushing around in a crowded place. Lotte felt small, not able to stand up and be the same height as everyone else. She disliked when people were late, but she would pay all the money she had to be able to rush through the corridors without a second thought.

In her current state she felt close to invisible to everyone around her; she felt as if she weren't there. Except for a girl standing over in a corner, popping her chewing gum over and over again, eyes glued to the wheelchair.

Lotte hurried to reach the elevator doors before they closed. "Hold the elevator!" she shouted.

Fajah's office was on the fifth floor, which meant that she would have to use the elevator to be able to get there. But it wasn't easy with people cutting in line and filling up the space until bursting. She waited a couple minutes until the elevator came back. On the second try, she managed to get inside, but from the glance of a man who could have easily chosen the stairs instead, she got the feeling that she took up too much space.

Fajah came and greeted her as soon as she reached her floor. The first thing Lotte noticed were the wide corridors, which made it easier for her to move around. The restroom also had a little wheelchair friendly sign on it, and all rooms were easy to access.

Lotte got a quick tour of the place with instructions on what to do that first day, which was to pack orders and make some calls, before they headed to Fajah's office.

"Thank you so much, this means a lot to me."

"Aw, no worries hun!" Fajah said, sitting down on top of her desk. "I needed a helping hand." She slurped loudly on her coffee, which seemed like something she often did.

"It's so cool that you have your own company. I looked at some of the clothes, they're all amazing!"

"It's been a long journey. It has been far from easy to build all this up." She waved her arm around at the things in her office, like the posters hanging on her wall, the mannequins standing next to them with sample clothes on and the many magazines in her bookshelves. "You know, me and Delilah only had a backpack each when we first arrived here from Ghana. That was it. She was fifteen and I was five," she said, putting her coffee mug aside and letting out a bitter laugh. "Lala basically raised me. But I guess we're even now, since I've played a big part in raising her son."

Their eyes met and there was a moment of silence.

Fiddling with the bracelets on her wrist, Fajah continued by saying, "As you may have noticed, Kenley's dad isn't really around much." She rose from her desk and walked over to a chair closer to Lotte. "I don't even know where the man is at the moment. Though, I'm pretty sure he and Lala broke up, *again*, a few months ago. To be honest, I'm waiting for them to get back together. And who really knows, maybe she even was at his place last night? She never came home." She remained silent for a few seconds and started to pick at her well polished pink nails as her bracelets now were in their right place. "I feel like I'm the only stable person Kenny has had around lately," she said, raising her chin and looking straight at Lotte. "I'm happy he has you."

Lotte turned her face away and tucked a strand of hair behind her ear. "You don't … You don't think it's weird that—"

"Oh, don't worry about that hun!" Fajah replied right away, knowing exactly what Lotte referred to. "Again, I feel bad saying it, but there is no chance they will last if she ever wakes up."

Lotte felt like a horrible person, almost feeling relieved hearing those words, *again*, from someone close to him. It made her feel less terrible about the situation. She also began to understand why Kenley acted the way he did. When she first learned about Joanne, Lotte felt like a cheap replacement. But maybe it was true that he fell out of love way before the crash occurred—at least she tried to tell herself that. Many would probably think it was morally wrong of Kenley to continue seeing Lotte, but it was a tricky situation and it felt like someone would get hurt no matter what happened. Lotte felt egoistic choosing to pursue what was best for her, but she wanted to feel happy, because that was something she hadn't felt in a long time.

Kenley made her feel that way.

During the day Lotte made some calls, scheduled a few meetings and organized a bunch of documents to be printed. She completed her assigned work for the day in just a few hours; she loved to organize and to get things done. Working for Fajah would give her another reason to get up in the mornings, something that would do her good.

※ ※ ※

Later that day, she sat on the countertop in the kitchen at Kenley's place, just like the day before. She looked out the tiny window and saw how twilight covered the sky like a duvet, as she waited for the alarm on her phone to go off. After she and Kenley had dinner, they decided to visit the grocery store to buy the ingredients he didn't have at home, so they could bake some Danish pastry together. They said it was to celebrate her successful first day at work, but they both knew; it was just another reason for Lotte to stay there longer.

As Lotte's phone started to play a little tune, Kenley grabbed the oven mitts and opened the oven. But what he didn't realize was that the oven mitts were threadbare on the left hand's thumb, so as he grabbed the incredibly hot baking tray, a tiny part of his bare skin touched it.

"Ah, crap!" He quickly put the baking tray at the top of the oven, then he turned on the tap and let the cool water run down his injured thumb.

Lotte fumbled to open the drawers she could reach from where she sat. "Where can I find a Band-Aid?"

"Oh, I'm not bleeding, it should be fine," he said while grimacing; it didn't bleed, but it burned and pulsated.

After a few seconds of searching, she found a small package with Band-Aids in it. A tiny yellow one with pink flowers on it caught her eye. "Come over here."

Kenley walked toward Lotte, hesitating. His forehead wrinkled, wondering what she was up to.

Lotte grabbed his hand. She blew some air on his thumb and gave it a smooch, before she put the Band-Aid on the newly injured part of his skin. "That's how my parents used to do when me or Lykke scratched our knees or elbows." Lotte giggled and said, "Worked every time."

He slowly drew what felt like an invisible heart with his thumb on the back of her hand. "You're right. It feels better already."

Lotte cupped his cheek, but she had completely forgotten that she still had baking flour on it, so a part of Kenley's cheek became covered with a powdery hand print. She tried to clean the mess she had caused, but she only made it worse and smeared it out even more.

He chuckled. "Don't worry about that, sweets."

The nickname rolling off his tongue made her heart hammer. Her lips formed a warm smile as she received another confirmation that the idea of something going on between them wasn't one sided.

A playlist mixed with calm African music, such as tones from djembe drums and balafons, together with relaxing jazz melodies played in the background, as they snuggled up in each other's arms in the kitchen, like they'd done the previous day. It felt as though there was a magnetic field between them, like some sort of force that pulled them closer to each other; it was hard to let go.

Burrowing his face in her neck and resting his head on her

shoulder, Kenley could feel, and almost hear, Lotte's heart bouncing inside of her chest in a steady rhythm; it was much better music to his ears than the sound coming from the speaker. He could listen on repeat for hours without getting tired of it.

But as one of the songs Fajah had sung along to in the car at least a thousand times when Kenley was younger started to play, he got an idea. He loosened his grip around Lotte and grabbed her hand instead. "May I have this dance?"

Her silence made him think that Lotte was looking at him in confusion, probably drawing her eyebrows closer together and most likely wrinkling her nose—which was exactly what she was doing.

Lotte removed his hand from hers. "You know I can't do that …"

"Of course you can!" Kenley reached for her wheelchair which stood a couple of meters away. "You have to keep an eye on me though, so I don't trip over something, or walk into the fridge," he said as he lifted her up and helped her down the kitchen counter.

She beamed at him, but tried not to sound so pleased when she said, "You know I charge a kiss every other minute for this type of torment, right?"

"Then it might get expensive for me, because I think you'll be surprised how fun it is." He walked toward the speaker and turned up the volume. "But it's worth it." Then he winked playfully in her direction.

Lotte would have lied if she said that she didn't like his goofy side. It was one more piece to the puzzle which she missed in her life. His not-so-graceful dance moves were hilarious to watch. He was far from talented, but somehow always managed to hit the right beats.

Dancing like he did in the kitchen that night was something Kenley never thought he would do. He'd barely danced in his life, had zero sense of rhythm and had always believed it would be incredibly embarrassing to do so in front of someone else.

"Dance with me!"

"I can't ... dance in this thing?" Lotte moved her wheelchair a bit back and forth. "It will look weird!" she exclaimed. She hunched her shoulders, looked down on her feet, and wished she were able to re-create one of those cute and romantic movie scenes, where the main character and the love interest danced until their feet were numb, in the refrigerator light, forgetting time and space.

"Well, it's not like I can see you?" he said, smiling broadly. It was clear that it pained him—he wanted to be able to, so badly. He could still only dimly see her contour through his eyes and wondering whether he would be able to see her one day was torture.

Kenley stepped closer to Lotte. He asked her to reach out her hand, which she did. He took her hand in his and brought it to his lips and kissed it, before lifting it up in the air. Lotte answered by spinning around in her wheelchair, doing a pirouette. Many times she needed that little extra push; Kenley was someone who challenged her to do things she never thought were possible.

She remembered how much Bernie had spoken about the *little things in life* and the joy they could bring. She didn't understand the depth of it at first, but after that evening in the kitchen, she finally could. It was the sheer bliss she felt when she was with him, the sparks flying between them which she could almost get a glimpse of with her eyes. It was the feeling of her lungs giving out from all the laughter at Kenley being Kenley. She imagined that she could live like that for an eternity.

The *little things* were greater than she'd thought.

But the question was: How long would the bliss last this time?

CHAPTER TWELVE

Lotte liked her new routine—getting up early and knowing she was needed somewhere. It was easier for her to get out of bed and she was much more productive in the mornings, since she had to leave the house at a certain time, to not be late for work.

The first few hours at the office she usually packed orders and in the afternoons she made a few calls and looked over Fajah's schedule for the coming days. When she was done for the day she called Kenley, to hear his voice and to let him know whether she was coming over or not. He usually always answered, but that day she reached his voice mail. She called him again a few minutes later, but he still didn't pick up. After waiting about twenty minutes, he still hadn't called her back. Maybe he'd fallen asleep? Lotte tried to push her worries aside, but since he told her that her calling him was one of the highlights of his day, it felt off that there was no one on the other end.

Fajah had to stay longer at work, so Lotte called her mom and asked if she could give her a ride to Kenley's place, which she could. When they arrived outside his apartment building, she looked up at the many windows facing the street. To her surprise, the tiny lamp on the window sill in the kitchen was off.

It was always on.

The door to the apartment was unlocked and it was quiet and dark, like in a horror movie, right before the scary creature is about to attack its prey. The door opened with a creak and she felt goosebumps cover her arms. As she looked into the apartment, the first thing she saw were several things lying on the floor—photo albums, newspapers, books, forks, spoons, along with the cup she'd used that morning—but it was no longer intact, its pieces spread out all over the floor.

The scene in front of her left her mouth wide open as a thousand thoughts flew around in her mind. Was she supposed to get help? What if someone had broken into the apartment?

"She's dead!" a trembling voice from inside the apartment cried out between sobs and screams.

Lotte went into the hallway, following the familiar voice. Her heart was beating hard and fast, like it could explode inside her chest any second. She continued further into the apartment, rushing from the hallway to the living room, where she startled, seeing Kenley sitting on the floor, in the dark, crying. Lotte's pulse increased rapidly as she saw him gasping for air, tears streaming down his face.

She felt the adrenaline pumping, but the bad kind.

Lotte hadn't done many transitions from her wheelchair to the floor by herself, but watching the scene unfold in front of her she didn't even hesitate; she almost threw herself onto it. She wouldn't feel any pain in her legs anyway.

When she was close enough, she removed Kenley's hands covering his face. "What's going on?" Lotte shrieked, breathing heavily.

"She's dead!" Kenley cried.

Lotte's accelerated heart rate made her feel nauseous and Kenley mumbling about death didn't make it any better. She couldn't think straight. "Who is dead?" Lotte shouted, tears filling her eyes, knowing the answer but needing to hear him say it.

"Joanne."

Lotte's heart shattered in as many pieces as the tea cup lying on the floor out in the hallway. She backed away in pure shock and put her hand to her mouth. The rest of her body felt as paralyzed as her legs. She had no idea what to say. In fact, there were no words that could make the situation better. Seeing Kenley biting his lip so hard that his teeth left marks to put a stop to the tears falling down was devastating. Seeing him digging his nails into the palm of his hand to move the pain elsewhere and hearing all the whimpers, made Lotte feel a terrible shooting pain in her chest. Worse than anything she'd ever felt in the days and months following her accident.

Lotte moved closer to Kenley. Her body was still shaky and her face drained of color. "It's not your fault," she whispered.

Kenley's voice was faltering as he said, "But I was behind the steering wheel." He took a short pause, failing to take a deep breath as he gathered his thoughts and continued: "Everyone blames me. Everyone blames me for her death."

"You couldn't have done anything more than what you did." Lotte put her hand on Kenley's cheek. "It wasn't your fault. Anyone with a brain understands that." She wiped away a tear falling down his cheek. "I know how hard it can be to maneuver a car. Especially in critical situations."

He tilted his forehead against hers, as they sat on the cold floor together, in the messy and dark apartment. The whole year had been a living in hell for Kenley. He saw only darkness and his thoughts were filled with flames which burned nearly all the beautiful memories he had left. Until she'd come into his life, and everything slowly got brighter and many of those flames were extinguished.

"I have not only one, but two shoulders you can cry on if you need to," she said, dragging her fingers through his curls. She knew it was a part of the secret recipe on how to make him calm; he had a soft spot for it. "I'm also incredibly stubborn. When I set my mind on something, it's hard to … change my opinion about it." She took a pause before she said, "I won't leave for a good while."

He let out a half-suppressed laugh. "Yeah I know. You are indeed very stubborn."

She moved her hand to his cheek once more. After a little while, he placed his on top of hers. At first she thought he would remove it, pull it down. But he didn't. Instead, he pressed his lips gently against the inside of her hand and gave it a kiss. He was exhausted, but his dimples were somewhat visible from the moon casting just enough light into the room, as he mumbled, "I would probably go insane if you weren't here."

Joanne had been in a coma for months, but now she was gone for good; he wouldn't ever be able to visit her at the hospital again. To Kenley, it for some reason still felt like she was a text message away. He'd been in denial all those months, trying to persuade himself it wasn't as bad as it seemed and that she would be okay one day, just like him.

It would most likely be a long grieving process ahead. But a part of him almost felt relieved that Joanne wouldn't feel any pain or have a limited life … that most of her last memories were good ones. He wished it all would have ended on a brighter note, but the past was the past.

Lotte pulled him closer and embraced him tightly. "I'm here for you," she said.

Kenley could hear her sniffling. He searched for her cheek with his hand and this time it was his turn to wipe away a few tears. Knowing *his problems* caused her pain made his heart bleed.

They stayed at the exact same spot on the floor for over an

hour. During that time, Lotte continued to hold him and run her fingers through his curls. Kenley was petrified, leaning against her, like he was frozen to the ground. It was only when his chest began rising and falling less rapidly and his tears had dried up, that she broke the silence and asked, "Do you want to go outside for a bit? We don't have to be out for long, but I ... think we both need to get some fresh air."

Answering with a nod, Kenley pulled away from her embrace and leaned against the sofa as he tried to stand up, his legs were rather wobbly. His arms felt like cooked spaghetti, but he tried his best to help Lotte back into her wheelchair before he dragged his feet toward the hallway and grabbed his jacket.

The aroma of coffee from the apartment was still stinging in his nostrils and his blood was still boiling. Sitting down on a bench in the park only a minute away from his apartment building, feeling the wind brush against his cheeks as he inhaled the fresh air, did wonders. But the most important thing to him was knowing Lotte sat next to him and that she wouldn't leave.

Kenley went to bed a couple of minutes after they came home. He was drained of energy after the day's events, which was understandable. Lotte's whole body felt limp and weak, but even though her eyelids were heavy, it was difficult for her to fall asleep. On the other side of the door, Delilah and Fajah walked back and forth, talking to each other with lowered and dejected voices for hours. Later, when the footsteps silenced, Lotte could relax and finally fall into a slumber herself.

Her brain had been working on overdrive the whole evening; as she finally closed her eyelids, she relived the memories she'd tried for so long to repress. She could see herself drowning in neon lights. She fell several times on her knees and tried to get up on her shaky legs, but it was hard when it felt like the floor was moving around beneath her. She made several attempts to talk to the people she was with, but they were too drunk to care, or simply couldn't hear over the music on the dance floor. Someone grabbed her by the waist and as she turned around, the guy who used to make her heart race stood in front of her. He gave her that intoxicating smile she later regretted she ever desired. Lotte wished she'd known earlier that Dalton would let her sink and that his words were just that—words without any meaning.

"Are you okay, sweets?" Kenley had woken up in the middle of the night from her quivering noises. He located her face with his hand and could feel the heat from her flushed cheeks.

Lotte opened her eyes a second after, frightened and startled. She held herself up on her elbows, before she realized it was only her mind playing tricks on her. Falling back onto the bed she exhaled deeply. "Sorry. I-I had a nightmare ..."

He caressed her left cheek with his thumb and after a while he asked, "Do you want to talk about it?"

"Now isn't a good time for that," Lotte replied, referring to the situation with Joanne. Talking about her past life wouldn't make things better.

Kenley moved closer to her and covered the parts of her body that weren't already under the duvet, in case she would start freezing in the middle of the night. "By the way, thank you for staying here tonight."

"Well, I like to sleep next to you, so I don't mind," she said, placing her head on his chest. "And, I'm a professional cuddler, so why not make the best out of my profession?"

He beamed at her in the dark, wishing he would be able to see her nestling up to him under the covers.

"I wish I could see you," he whispered.

"Oh believe me, I look like a troll right now."

"A cute troll then?" he said, imagining her hair spread out in all directions over the pillow she rested her head on. That would have been a sight for sore eyes.

That night was only the third time they'd fallen asleep next to each other, but Lotte wouldn't have wanted it any other way. She adored their pillow talks and felt important and needed when she was with him. The past days had brought them a lot closer, but Lotte wished it didn't involve Joanne taking her last breath. Seeing Kenley's reaction made her feel a sort of pain she'd never felt before, and she began to worry about how the situation would affect their future together.

Sometime later, in the middle of the night, there was a distant sound of sirens coming from down the street. It made Kenley's heart pick up speed. The noise died down fast, but it made him toss and turn for the rest of the night anyway. He held his arm around Lotte, so he could feel her presence—like he was afraid they would drift apart in an endless ocean if he didn't.

He was paranoid he would lose her as well.

CHAPTER THIRTEEN

Fajah let Lotte take a few days off from work, to look after Kenley while she and Delilah were away from home. She felt a bit guilty about it, since she'd only recently started working for the company, but Fajah reassured her that it was much more important to be with Kenley than it was packing orders.

The day after Joanne passed away was heart wrenching for Lotte to witness. Kenley cried, and cried, nonstop. He barely left his room. As the shock of Joanne being gone forever began to subside, all the feelings he'd tried to suppress the night before came back to slap him in the face.

The second day was better. Together, Lotte and Fajah, managed to get him out on a walk. She and Kenley shared some meaningful conversations together, to encourage him to let all his feelings out. Delilah drifted in and out, grabbing a few things from the kitchen, saying good morning, and trying to avoid eye contact. She hadn't met Lotte properly yet, and made no attempt to that day. It made Lotte feel like an intruder, like she wasn't welcome there in Delilah's presence. But Lotte understood that the situation was hard to cope with, for anyone.

A few days later, they'd arranged an extra session with the

group, to make sure Kenley got the support he needed. Kenley wasn't sure at first if he wanted to go, but Lotte convinced him, almost sounding like her own mother when she'd first tried to convince Lotte to join the support group sessions.

Kenley had bags under his eyes, his curls were a bit tousled, he forgot to put on the watch he always wore on his wrist and he didn't care what clothes he was wearing—something he usually put thought into. Instead he'd picked something that felt comfortable, an old sweater and a pair of sweatpants. Even though he might have looked like a mess, his mind felt lighter than he thought it would, only three days after Joanne's death. Most likely because of the woman he leaned his head against in the car, who made sure to comb his curls for him, carried his watch in her pocket and made his life feel meaningful despite everything. She picked up the pieces and tried to glue them back together.

With the whole group gathered again, Bernie felt left out. Like he'd been missing out on some important information, especially after seeing Lotte and Kenley sitting so close, with not much space between them. Bernie glanced at Nova who nodded in response and tried to explain everything that had happened lately with weird and rapid movements with her hands, moving her lips like she was talking, without saying a word—in an attempt to be discreet, which she wasn't. She wasn't discreet at all.

Bernie cleared his throat to break the morose silence. "Good to see everyone again. So, who wants to start with sharing something, anything, you have experienced this last week?"

Ian looked at Nova, Nova looked at Lotte, Lotte looked at Ian, Kenley faced the floor. Nova and Ian were afraid they in some way would offend Kenley by sharing the highlights of their past days.

Kenley held Lotte's hand in a strong grip, his muscles were still a bit tense but his breathing became calmer for every minute that passed, and his thoughts more collected. To everyone's surprise, he said, "I-I can start." He could imagine four pairs of shocked eyes looking his way.

Bernie leaned forward despite being taken aback. "We're all ears."

"I just wanted to ... thank all of you for helping me through some really difficult times." He took a short pause, trying to hold back his tears. "Especially ... you, Lotte." Kenley turned his head to his right at the same time as she turned hers to the left. "Thank you for keeping me sane."

She wanted to say the same thing to him, but she felt tongue-tied.

Kenley continued, "Since my accident, I feared getting close to someone again. I was afraid I would hurt that person. But, being with you is something I will never regret." His mood lightened as he thought about the joy Lotte had brought him lately. "I may be almost completely blind, but you have made me see things in a new light and it feels like I *can* actually see the beauty you describe. I can paint the pictures in my mind." Beaming in her direction, he said, "You've been splashing color to my black and white life since the first day we met."

Hearing him say all those things about her made her heart feel full. She kissed him on the shoulder, before resting her forehead against it, not caring that the others were watching.

She had a way with words, but she'd always struggled with telling people how much they meant to her. Lotte usually showed it in her actions instead. She hoped Kenley knew how she felt and that she had proven enough through her kisses and touches to convince him.

Bernie wished more than anything that all four people in front of him one day would feel free from their pasts. He himself had lived through many dark times in his life, times when he felt like nothing he did turned out the way he wanted. Seeing Lotte and Kenley embrace each other, he decided to share his own story.

Bernie's wife had struggled with depression for many years and when she was finally on the road to recovery, the next tragedy came. They hadn't had any luck at first when it came to starting a family together. After years of trying, they still stood without a baby while all their friends had kids of their own. It made his wife fall back into the mental state she was in when she was at her worst; it had been one of the most dreadful experiences of Bernie's life. He'd never felt like more of a failure. The woman he loved most shed tears every day and was losing strength. On top of that, he'd almost lost his job from spending so much time at home, caring for her. He lay awake at night, thinking of everything that had gone wrong; he couldn't stop worrying about when the other shoe would drop.

It took him a while—precisely four kids and soon five grand-kids—to realize that he could help others. Help others, who felt like the whole world was against them, to see the beauty of life again.

When he could only see darkness, he wished he'd had someone to talk to. Someone who wouldn't look at him like he was about to go insane. Someone he could relate to, to feel less alone. His friends and brothers hadn't understood what he'd felt, but he couldn't blame them. After all, they'd never gone through something similar.

Bernie felt a lot of responsibility for the four other people in the room; he would never give up on them. He wanted them to be able to talk about their struggles with one another, because opening up was important. His goal was to see Nova back in the saddle, make Ian dream about his future, make sure Kenley stopped having nightmares and see Lotte gain her confidence back. But also, for them to have life-long friends in each other.

The reason Bernie chose to share the final details this day was because thunderstorms *could* end with sunshine. Bernie thought it was especially important to share this with Kenley, who not only saw darkness in his mind, but also through his eyes.

Lotte nodded along to what Bernie told them. She felt the lump in her throat get bigger, so she tried to clear it quietly. Being the one in pain, as well as being the one watching the suffering from the sidelines, were things she could relate to.

One of the things he told them hit close to home for Lotte, especially. She lost more than her career and the ability to feel her legs that day of the crash. There was more to the story, something only she knew—something she imagined she would carry with her to the grave. She had definitely not planned on letting the secret out, especially not during the current circumstances, but about an hour and a half into the session, two of Bernie's grandkids stormed into the room, changing everything.

"You two! You know what I said about running in here like that." Bernie tried to sound firm, but it was hard for him to do so, as they jumped around him and giggled.

A woman, who must have been their mom, walked quickly into the room and apologized for the sudden interruption. She gave everyone in the room a compassionate look, hoping that her kids hadn't disturbed them too much. She tried to make them leave the room with her, but the youngest ran and hid behind Nova the same time as the eldest started to discuss her love for crocus flowers with Kenley. The little girl talking to him had beautiful brown eyes and dark curly hair, just like his.

Great.

Many would probably swoon seeing someone they were dating—or whatever their relationship was—interacting with a kid, but Lotte only felt her chest become heavy. The thought that she would most likely never be able to have the family she'd always dreamed of, broke her.

Feeling as sensitive as she had been after the previous nights, talking about kids made her feel incredibly vulnerable; it was hard to hold back the tears. She told the others she had to use the restroom, but once she closed the door behind her and sat alone in the lobby, tears ran down her cheeks uncontrollably.

The door creaked behind her and Kenley stepped out. "Are you okay? Nova said you looked sad?" He searched after the sofa with his cane and when he located it, he sat down in front of her. "I'm sorry about this whole thing with Joanne."

At first Lotte wanted to pretend she was only crying because of the Joanne-situation, but keeping her secret only to herself had been much harder lately. Besides, she didn't want Kenley to think his "problems" caused her more pain than they did.

"No one, literally no one, knows about this. So please keep this between us," she said, faint as a whisper.

Kenley raised his head and with furrowed brows he turned in her direction, trying to understand what he'd missed, as Lotte gathered some courage before speaking freely about something she'd kept to herself since the crash.

How she'd opened her heart to a tiny human she never got to meet in person. One that she'd seen on a white and black monitor screen, heartbeat ticking, only a few weeks before her accident.

One she had lost along with everything else.

CHAPTER FOURTEEN

Sitting curled up in Kenley's arms on the sofa in the still empty and quiet lobby, the only sounds that could be heard were Lotte's soft whimpers.

"You've kept all of that to yourself?" he asked.

"I felt ashamed. I didn't want people to … be even more worried. The wheelchair and all the complications were enough as it were."

She was planning on telling her boyfriend the news after the race, but the opportunity never came. Instead she ended up lying almost lifeless on the ground, next to what was left of her car.

In her opinion, Dalton didn't deserve to know either, since he'd left as soon as he could.

Kenley, on the other hand, kept her closer and held her tighter, which was one of the major differences. She'd been scarred by her previous relationships. But time after time, Kenley proved that she'd fallen for the wrong men earlier in her life; one red flag after another, compared to Kenley's green.

After about half an hour, the door creaked again. Nova peeked into the lobby from a few meters away. Ian was right behind her, pushing Nova aside as he ran toward Lotte to give her a hug.

Nova made her best attempt to reach her before him. From afar it looked like the beginning of a wrestling match.

Ian got to the sofa first and pulled them into a group hug. "Nova and I are like parasites, sorry to break it to you ..."

A few seconds later, Nova joined them. "We're here for you, whether you want it or not!"

Lotte thought Kenley's grimace at being sandwiched in the hug was adorable and it was impossible not to smile over the fact that she was lucky to have people like Nova and Ian in her life.

She giggled and hugged them back.

Nova glanced at Lotte and with an overly serious tone of voice she asked, "So, who gives better hugs, me or Ian?"

*　*　*

The blue sky was covered with dark, heavy clouds as Lotte waited outside the building for her dad to come and pick her up; it could start to rain any minute.

Kenley came walking up behind her under the streetlight. He fiddled nervously with the band sitting on the handle of his cane. "Let me know if you need anything, okay?"

"Do you want to come over to my house?" Lotte tried to read his face in the dim light, in case he showed any sign of doubt. "I don't want to be alone," she said, almost whispering.

"I would love to. I don't have any things with me now though. So, maybe I can come over in an hour or so once Fajah picks me up from here?"

"Sounds great. Thanks."

He kneeled and faced her, hoping their eyes were almost at the same level. "You don't have to thank me, sweets."

Lotte's dad pulled up down the street and honked the horn several times, since he knew Lotte found that extremely embarrassing. As Rasmus had predicted, she rolled her eyes and made gestures with her hand, telling him to stop acting like someone who had the mental age of a fifteen-year-old.

"So uh, see you later!" she said as she headed toward the car. But after a few meters she stopped to cast a brief look over her shoulder, back at Kenley, who'd started putting on his jean jacket as it had become chilly. How blessed was she? Not only would she probably be able to borrow that comfortable-looking jacket one day, but it felt like she'd won the jackpot, having him in her life. He was like the cherry on the top of her sundae, the ketchup to her french fries—simply the feeling of the weekend coming.

Only knowing him for a short period of time almost made her feel bad for not sharing her secrets with the people she'd known her whole life. As it was, she knew that evening she would just tell her family she'd had a bad day, which was something she'd perfected over the years—keeping everything inside.

* * *

Rain was pattering against the floor-to-ceiling windows in Lotte's room. They weren't all covered with curtains, so each time a flash of lightning struck, the whole room lit up. She used to flinch at the booming sounds of a thunderstorm. She used to stay awake and count the seconds after she saw the sky light up, to know how far away it really was. She used to cover her ears as the sounds triggered painful memories. But having Kenley beside her made it easier to cope with. To her surprise, it was even a bit cozy. She wasn't alone.

She felt safe.

Her heart felt much lighter not having to carry her miscarriage all by herself; the weight had clearly gotten to be too much to handle. She'd been waiting for someone who wouldn't judge her for keeping it to herself all those months; someone whose words made her blush in the dark, someone who kissed the scar on her cheek, someone who kept the smile on her lips a little while longer.

Someone like Kenley.

Lotte had been debating if she should tell him how much she appreciated him. It probably didn't hurt to be extremely clear, to make sure what she wanted didn't slip through her fingers.

He was lying behind her, stroking her hair in slow movements, while Lotte was staring through the big windows, watching the rain hammer against them. "I appreciate you ... and like you a lot," she said, not facing him.

Kenley suddenly stopped stroking her hair and lifted himself up onto his elbow. "Good, because there is no one I would rather steal duvets from," he said while gripping the duvet, pulling it toward him.

Kenley could feel her turning around to look at him. He could picture the scene in his mind—her pulling her eyebrows together out of curiosity, her head slightly tilted to the side.

He continued, "I can't help it, you know. You're like yogurt. You make everything better." Kenley swore he heard her trying to dampen that sweet laugh of hers, so he proceeded by saying, "I've fallen for you and I can't get up!" Then he threw himself back onto the bed with a thud.

Lotte hovered her upper body over him. "Yogurt? Of all things?" She tried to sound annoyed, but the smile on her face kind of ruined the way the words came out of her mouth.

Kenley found her face with his hand and drew his fingers from her chin, up along her jawline, until he found her cheek. "Eh, you know how much I like yogurt, so that's a compliment."

Lotte traced her fingertips up and down his chest in tender movements in an invisible pattern. Moving her hand further up to his collarbone and neck he started to get goosebumps under her touch.

"Well that tickles!"

She gave him a devilish smirk he couldn't see; waited a few seconds, and started to tickle him under his armpit.

"Are you attacking me?" Kenley rolled around, squealing, trying to defend himself. "If I were you, I would stop!" he exclaimed between laughs.

She grinned against his mouth. "Make me."

In one swift movement, she was the one who became trapped under him. He gave her a mischievous grin—a warning that he would give her a taste of her own medicine.

Sounding unbothered, Lotte said, "Well, good luck. I'm not ticklish!" She bit her lower lip, trying not to give in too quickly as she was letting his fingertips wander over her body the way she had done to him.

Her not giving him the reaction he wanted made Kenley start placing kisses on her neck. It affected her senses more than she wanted to confess. He always managed to cover her skin with goosebumps and make her desperate for more. He knew it would work. He knew how to pierce her heart and how to tattoo his touch onto her body and mind.

Damn nerve endings.

"Breaking the rules already, I see? Does that mean I won?" she asked, feeling his lips curve into a smile against her neck.

Right into her ear, he whispered, "You're a tough one, I ran out of ideas. And I really want to kiss you, so …"

Her heart was clapping rapidly inside her chest from his lips against her bare skin—from him being so close, with almost no air between them. "Kiss me then," she said as she pulled his head closer, making their noses brush against each other.

He chuckled, sending a shiver down her spine, before he closed the last bit of distance between them.

To her, kissing him felt like heaven and him deepening the kiss made her feel like she was in paradise. Their entangled bodies made her feel like she was melting ice cream on a hot summer's day—a summer she definitely didn't want to end.

* * *

Lotte's mom, Karla, had attended several courses, learning how to give her daughter proper therapeutic massages. It partially compensated for her lack of movement, it helped the blood flow better and it also reduced the risk of painful muscle contractions.

She smeared her hands with some moisturizer as she walked toward the massage table Lotte was lying on, inside the spare room they had transformed into a home spa. "So, when are you going to admit that I was right?"

Lotte raised her head and looked at her mom in confusion. "Right about what?"

She began to massage her strained shoulders. "Going to therapy." It was hard for her to keep it together when she noticed her daughter giving her the side-eye.

Lotte grunted, knowing that her mom would for sure tease her for that as long as Kenley was around, to prove once again that she was always right.

"Oh, or maybe that he spent the night in the guest room?" Karla implied. "Maybe I read the situation completely wrong and missed when he walked out of—"

Lotte let out a cry before she said, "Why are all three of you so curious about my love life? It's concerning!"

"We care about you, skat. That's why!"

The door out to the hallway was slightly open. Lotte could hear her sister and her dad being overly annoying, grilling Kenley with questions as they ate breakfast. They asked everything from what his favorite color was to what he expected to achieve in the coming years. Lykke hadn't planned on visiting that week, but when Lotte told her Kenley was going to be there, she showed up faster than lightning.

"Relax …" Karla could feel Lotte's muscles becoming more tense. She closed the door with her foot to shut out the conversation in the kitchen. "The worst thing they can do is start singing out of nowhere or maybe tell him weird things you did as a baby."

"Well that would be awful, since I can't defend my past actions when I'm in *here*."

Her mom backed away from the massage table in protest. "If you could please relax your body, I'll make sure we're done in fifteen minutes, okay?"

"Deal," Lotte muttered.

Those fifteen minutes were painfully long and the door being closed only turned the voices from the kitchen into faint whispers to her. She hoped Kenley wasn't too weirded out just yet by her family's odd, but also somehow endearing, behaviors.

* * *

"So, to answer the most important question of them all …" Lykke took a dramatic pause before she continued by asking, "Do you like pineapple on your pizza?"

Lotte watched them interact from a few meters away when her mom had finished with her massage. So far, it looked like they were having a peaceful conversation at the kitchen table, which was a huge relief.

Kenley chuckled at Lykke's question and replied, "I prefer to eat pineapple in a bowl, next to the pizza."

Lykke's eyes widened. "Oh … I've never heard that one before." She rubbed her chin. "Interesting …" she said, sounding like a detective searching for clues.

As soon as she saw that Lotte was trying to blend in with the wall, she gave her sister a thumbs up, whispering loudly on purpose, so everyone in the room heard it, "Psst! Lotte? We like him!" She nodded at their dad who sat next to her—and he also gave Lotte a thumbs up.

Kenley turned around and faced Lotte. That cute smile of his that showed the gap between his front teeth and his dimples, was something she would never get tired of seeing. Suddenly the idea of growing old and wrinkly didn't seem so bad after all.

Rasmus grinned at Lykke, as though he was asking for backup for what he was about to say. "Kenley, do you want to hear stories about Lotte's rebellious teen years?"

"We have plenty, she was wild!" Lykke claimed, smirking at her sister.

Kenley was quick to respond, "I want to hear them all!"

Just like that, Lotte wanted the ground beneath her to swallow her whole.

CHAPTER FIFTEEN

A week used to feel like a month back then when Lotte never left her house, especially when all she ever did was stare at the ceiling in her room. She used to have so much time that she counted each second that passed. But suddenly a week flew by—so fast, that she almost wished the clock would stop ticking, at least for a little while. She made calls, organized papers and packed orders from early mornings until late afternoons. After work she spent time with Kenley, or hung out with her family, since the four of them had started spending more time together again.

It was Friday afternoon and Lotte had ended her last shift of the week. Fajah gave her a ride on her way home and dropped her off outside Kenley's apartment building. Lotte entered the well-memorized pin code, which opened the door to the building for her. Once inside, she took the familiar elevator to the third floor, and wheeled herself to the first apartment to her right. She rang the doorbell, but Kenley wasn't the one who opened the door. For once, Delilah was home.

Lotte was taken by surprise and the only thing that came out of her mouth was a vague, "Hi."

Delilah didn't look too pleased to see Lotte at her doorstep.

"Hello," she said as she let go of the door handle and walked back into the kitchen. She looked over her shoulder shortly after and added, "I guess you already know where his room is?"

The way Delilah said it made it sound like Lotte was only there for one thing only. "Y-yeah, I do."

Lotte took a quick peek inside the kitchen as she passed by. Delilah was scrubbing the counter top almost violently and placing all cups, plates and cutlery in their correct spots.

"Do you need help with anything?" Lotte asked.

Delilah shook her head as she continued to scrub the—already shining—counter top. "No, no. It's fine."

Lotte kept replaying the moments from the times she and Delilah had been in the same room in her mind, trying to figure out what she'd done wrong. Maybe it was something she'd said? Or maybe it was the fact that she and Kenley had gotten too close too fast for her liking. Maybe Delilah and Joanne knew each other well? Maybe Delilah thought Kenley moved on too quickly and didn't grieve her death enough? He was for sure still grieving, but mostly behind closed doors. There were nights when he cried himself to sleep and other times when he woke up because of nightmares in which Joanne appeared.

Kenley's mood since her passing had been a series of ups and downs. Some days, he felt numb, nothing. Some days, he was incredibly overwhelmed and wanted to break things. Some days he wished everything was an illusion and that her heart was still beating. But most days, he managed the feelings better than he'd ever imagined he would. Probably since he'd already "lost" her right after the accident, and that was months ago. He had to accept his new reality, that she was gone forever. There was nothing he could do about it.

Done was done.

* * *

Long shadows covered the ground in front of them as they entered a park under the blaze of the evening sky. It was windy and a bit cooler outside, since they'd entered November and approached the winter months, but the temperature was milder than usual for that time of year.

It was late, but not late enough for the "fun-day-sports-day" to be in full swing, with people of all ages in the park. There was a mini golf course, mini tennis nets and football goals—a few ponies were there too. She could also see a couple of soapbox cars in the distance. It was quite lively. The kids ran around trying out different sports, the parents either playing with them, or chasing after them. But further away from all the chaos, there was one empty bench.

Overthinking was something Lotte often did; the situation with Kenley's mom was no exception. She couldn't stop dragging around the tiny charm on her necklace. "I don't think your mom likes me," she said.

Kenley leaned forward, rested his forearms on his legs and turned his head toward her. "Why do you say that?"

"She never wants to talk to me, she keeps our conversations short, she doesn't look me in the eye … It feels like she wants me to leave the room when I'm at your place," Lotte explained.

Moving closer, he put his arm around Lotte. Kenley had apologized on his mom's behalf a few times already. Hearing that Delilah had been so bitter, not making Lotte feel welcome, wasn't fun for him to learn. Kenley had hoped that his parents getting back together would help at least a little bit, but clearly it hadn't. He wasn't fully convinced they were seeing each other again, but Kenley had heard his dad was back in town.

"I know it might be hard, but please don't think you're doing anything wrong. It's my mom who's acting weird." Kenley sighed and rubbed the nape of his neck. "Fajah adores you—and so do I.

That's the most important thing." He gave her a kiss on the side of her forehead. "Mom better get used to you being around."

Lotte leaned her head against his shoulder. "I hope so, because since I met you, I've smiled more than I ever used to." She beamed before continuing, "Sometimes before I fall asleep at night, my face almost hurts from smiling. I-I mean, hurts in a good way!" Looking up at him, she could see a very pleased look on his face.

A soft breeze carrying the scents from a nearby snack- and smoothie stall swept past where they sat, which made Kenley realize they hadn't eaten dinner yet. "Do you want anything to eat or drink? It's on me."

"A sandwich and a smoothie or something would be nice."

"Okay, I'll go and buy that for you then. I'll be back in a few minutes," Kenley said. Then he stood up and unfolded his cane.

Sounding more worried than intended, she asked him, "Are you sure you'll manage it alone?"

He smiled at her, making those creases in his cheeks she loved visible. "I don't know. But I'm in for the challenge." Then he walked away, following the directions Lotte had given him.

But before he rounded a bush next to the bench Lotte sat on, he stopped and turned around—wishing more than anything that he could see those hazel eyes shimmer in the golden hour light, at least once in his life.

* * *

On the way to the park, Lotte had completely missed the big signs and posters that were placed around the city, about the race which would take place the coming week. It was only later on she realized the soapbox cars in the park weren't a coincidence.

She knew very well that the city they lived in had a racing track; she had memorized the whole route, even though she knew she would never be able to race through it herself. She'd heard on the news that people she used to know had stood on the podium after mastering that very route—but she never expected the most familiar face of them all to show up to challenge the throne anytime soon.

Dalton had tried his best to avoid Lotte as much as he could. It seemed unlikely that he would be at a place where there was a risk of them bumping into each other. That was why, at first, Lotte thought she was hallucinating when she noticed the man walking toward her had an oddly familiar gait, hairstyle and full-sleeve tattoos. The tattoos were visible as he was carrying his jacket in his hand, despite the chilly evening—typical of him to show off every moment he could.

In the corner of her eye she could see the man who'd bought her expensive diamond earrings—despite her not having any piercings—approaching. She tried to pretend she didn't see him by shifting the focus to her phone. But it got harder and harder the closer he came and she could feel her heart rate increase rapidly and her palms become sweaty. She had thought of many things she'd scream at his face if she ever got the chance, but her mind went blank as she saw him standing only three meters away.

"Lotte? I didn't know you were a park-person?"

She continued to look down on her phone and exhaled deeply. "I didn't know that about you either."

"A few of my mates and I try to recruit some of the kiddos over there. We're advertising a bit for next week's race. I'm kind of on the clock. I have to be here."

Giving him some sort of half-smile, she looked up at him and hissed, "Go and do your work then." Then she continued to scroll through the photo album on her phone.

Dalton smirked at her, like he enjoyed being above her. "So, what's up?"

"Nothing much. Clearly." Lotte could almost feel her veins

pulsating. Keeping the conversation civil would for sure be a challenge. "What about you?"

"Things are going well at the moment, I can't complain," he said with a chuckle, but silenced it short afterwards when he noticed Lotte's disinterest in him. "Oh, stop giving me that look!"

She wanted to lash out on him. "It's hard not to. To be honest, I don't want to see you right now."

"I loved you." For the first time in a minute he didn't maintain eye contact. He looked past her instead as he said, "Goddamnit, I still do!"

She wanted to smash something. "If you loved me as much as you claim, then tell me how it was possible for you to continue the race, and receive that trophy with a smile on your face, like nothing had happened?"

"But Lotte, babe, you know I had to finish what I'd started—"

She wanted to lose her temper. "If you'd been the one lying on the ground, lifeless, I would have stopped my car. I wouldn't even have hesitated." She took a deep breath, trying to swallow the frustration in the hope of being the bigger person, but her voice was trembling. "I get it's not easy to stop a car during a race, but if you love me as much as you say, I truly wonder why it took you so many hours to show up at the hospital."

Dalton's eyes narrowed and he crossed his arms over his chest as he tried to justify his actions. "I-I came as soon as I could!"

"I know you were partying, so now, get out of my sight." Lotte leaned back on the bench, attempting to shoo him away with her hand, doing her best to avoid looking at him.

Lotte and Dalton never came out with their relationship publicly. People speculated and gossiped, whether they were together or not, but they never confirmed anything. They'd been spotted outside walking together once or twice, but they never attended any events. Everything to be able to be alone, be under the radar, a chance to get away from the spotlight. But that was what made it easy for Dalton to claim nothing was going on between them to the media after everyone found out about Lotte's paraplegia. That was also why he didn't get much hate for it, since most people bought that they'd never dated and believed the sympathetic messages he'd spread all over the internet.

"Is everything okay here?" Kenley asked, as he came walking around the bush after overhearing the last part of the conversation.

Lotte grabbed the smoothie cup which Kenley reached out to her. "Thank you, *skat*."

Dalton got the hint and began to walk away from them. "She's not easy to be with," he scoffed.

"Meh, I thought I was the blind one?" Kenley took a sip of his coffee and slurped loudly, the same way Fajah did.

Lotte almost spit out the smoothie she had in her mouth. Seeing Dalton's baffled face as he looked over his shoulder back at them was priceless; it gave her the feeling that she was ahead of him on the leaderboard.

*　*　*

Talking to Dalton and seeing the soapbox cars made Lotte realize she hadn't visited her friend Edward and his garage in a month. She used to stop by every other week, if not weekly. Not feeling the same longing to sit behind the steering wheel in her old racing car, was probably because of the new and more exciting things happening in her life. The garage was still an important place for her though. Bringing Kenley there was at the top of her to-do list. So, one afternoon when they had nothing else to do, they decided to take the bus to visit Edward.

As they got closer to the old, white rectangular building, a whiff of gasoline and engine oil mixed with the cold air filled their nostrils. There was something about the familiar smell that made Lotte feel at home.

It had only been a month since she last visited, but somehow the facade of the building in front of her looked a lot more aged. It was dirty, like it hadn't been cleaned in ages. On top of that, the vegetation around the place grew at an extreme pace, making the garage look desolate from the outside. She'd never seen the garage from that perspective before.

"If it isn't the Devil herself?" Carrying a car wheel in his arms, Edward came walking toward them. "It's been a while!"

"Should you really be carrying that, old man?" Lotte asked, pointing to the heavy-looking item.

Edward put it down on the ground in front of him and stretched his back. "I probably shouldn't. It's not easy to accept that almost all my hair is white now."

Edward, or Eddie as she called him, had been Lotte's mentor through the early years of her racing career. He'd taught her how to drive, had always been around teaching her new tricks and helped taking care of her cars. Edward was the one who taught Lotte that girls could play with cars as well as boys. He'd turned into an extra grandpa, which made Lotte even more worried when she saw how much paler and slimmer he had become since she'd last seen him.

Eddie sighed in relief. "Good to see you again, Lotte." His eyes shifted to Kenley. "And oh ... who's your friend?"

"I'm Kenley, nice to meet you," he said.

Eddie beamed at her before he turned around to grab the car key. He opened a little cabinet hanging on the wall, grabbed the key to Lotte's car and tossed the keychain into the air until it landed in her hands.

"Thirty minutes. No more." Eddie gave her a serious look, the smile on his lips disappearing, before he walked away to continue the repairs on an old car.

Eddie was talking from experience, since Lotte always came back with tears in her eyes after feeling the steering wheel with her hands. But the last time she was in his garage, there had still been a deep and empty hole the racing had left behind. The weeks in between, something else had started to fill that empty void more and more, which now showed, since seeing the shimmering red and white car in front of her with the text "Danish Dynamite" spray-painted on it, didn't hurt as much as it used to.

After moving from her wheelchair to the driver's seat, she drummed with her fingers on the steering wheel. "This was my first car actually."

Kenley joined her and sat down next to her in the passenger seat. "What color is it? I think I could glimpse something red?"

"It's red and white." She looked over at Kenley, instead of staring at the grayish cement wall on the other side of the windshield. "My racing suits used to be that color too." She giggled. "Just like the Danish flag."

"I can imagine that red is your color," he said, making the blood flowing in Lotte's cheeks increase abruptly.

"I remember driving through Denmark, Sweden and Germany in this car—letting my hair loose, windows down and blasting music." She looked at her own reflection as she adjusted the rearview mirror. "Fun times," Lotte said as she tried to reach the gas pedal with her foot—but no muscle in her lower body wanted to cooperate.

Kenley faced Lotte and searched for her hand, which he eventually grabbed. "If I ever get my sight back and dare to get a new driver's license," he began, "I promise to take you on a ride in this very car and drive through Denmark, Sweden and Germany —windows down with the music blasting."

She intertwined their fingers, before lifting his hand to her lips, giving it a kiss.

***

They stayed in the car for a while. Lotte took a moment to feel the gear stick in her hand, turn the steering wheel and look at the several stickers she'd put on the interior. She was well aware there existed options for her if she really wanted to drive again one day. But sitting still in a car that didn't move was one thing; she had full control. Thinking about it now, really deeply thinking about it, she wasn't sure whether she would ever be able to drive again. Not because of her paraplegia, but because of the mental obstacles inside her head. Loud noises, like wheels screeching against asphalt or loud bangs—even thunder—were enough for her to feel sick and want to lie in a fetal position. At the same time, she was coming to terms with the fact that one chapter of her life had ended, and another recently had started.

"So ... Devil?" Kenley asked.

She snapped out of her thoughts, and replied, "It was my nickname ... What people expected me to be." Fidgeting with the seat belt, she continued by saying, "But after a while ... I kind of slowly, unconsciously, turned into that person." Remembering her regrets and all the stupid things she'd done during her career made her frown, almost shut her eyes, like the memories were flashing by right in front of her. "It isn't something I'm proud of. The pressure was ... too much sometimes."

She glanced over at Kenley who sat silent beside her. She stiffened and tilted her upper body slightly forward to be able to take in his reaction. It was first when a small smile appeared on his face she could relax and lean back into her seat again. "As long as you learn and grow from your mistakes," he assured.

With a grunt she said, "It might be hard to believe, but I have made a few people cry."

"You were that scary, eh? Do you have fangs or something?"

She shoved his arm gently with her hand.

Kenley reached for her cheek with his hand and looked at the very blurry version of her face. "At least I know what's behind that facade of yours."

It was intimate moments like those she loved. Especially the feeling of their hearts lingering, coming together for a little longer —a little closer each time. They were far from perfect, but they complemented each other and made two broken pieces into one whole. She knew they would go through seasons and that the endless daydreaming about him from daybreak to deepening twilight would fade over time, but she wanted to let that spark of new love live for as long as possible.

She leaned in and kissed him on the lips, but was interrupted in the midst of it when Eddie knocked on the car window and fake-coughed outside to get their attention.

Lotte quickly removed her hand that had found its way under Kenley's shirt and cleared her throat before she pushed the button to wind down the window by the driver's seat. "What?"

"First of all … time is up." Eddie leaned against the car and exhaled loudly. "And ugh, no love making in my garage, thanks!"

"We were literally just kissing!" she exclaimed.

"Ah ah ah! I know how young people behave," Eddie claimed. "Hormones everywhere!" He muttered something they couldn't hear as he turned his back on them and walked away.

Kenley tried his best to hold back his laughter until Lotte pushed the button to bring the car window up again. "What have you done in the poor man's garage to make him so worried?" he asked.

She dropped her head with a thud against the steering wheel, making the sound from the honking horn shriek through the whole garage. "Nothing, I swear. Literally nothing!" But on the other hand, she and Dalton used to hook up in the back of their cars every other business day, or in the driver's seat if they were in a hurry—so maybe he hadn't got it all wrong after all.

His words echoed throughout the building as he yelled, "Not in my garage!"

To annoy him, Lotte honked the horn a few more times with her palm.

In response, Eddie put two fingers together from both hands behind his head, making it look like two devil horns.

Lotte grinned back at him.

Some things never change.

CHAPTER SIXTEEN

A few more weeks had passed and at this point, Lotte was spending more nights at Kenley's place than in her own home. Her stuff was all over his desk, the pantry was loaded with chocolate powder for her milk at breakfast, she used his charger for her phone every other day and he'd recently widened the threshold into his room.

She'd been feeling incredibly comfortable lately—almost too comfortable. Sitting on the dark marble vanity top in the bathroom as they got ready for bed one night, Lotte wore a tank top with no bra, sleep shorts and her hair tied in a messy bun on her head. It wasn't like Kenley could see it, but he could probably feel that she didn't cover up as much skin as she used to.

Lotte brushed her teeth as she watched Kenley attempting to shave his face. The walls in the bathroom were dark gray and the only lit lamp was above the golden edged mirror behind her, making it quite dark—but it did cast a dreamy glow over the room. More light would probably not help him much anyway, since the blurry layer that covered his sight was like a foggy wall most times—at least it created a cozy atmosphere for Lotte. The small goldish flower pots filled with pink flowers scattered around the bathroom, together with the fragrance of lavender in the air, was a cherry on top.

Kenley leaned with his hands against the vanity top, intensely staring at the mirror, hoping to see his reflection. But as always, he didn't.

"You missed a spot." Lotte grabbed the razor from Kenley's hand before he had the opportunity to put it to the side. Then she carefully dragged it over the part of his cheek where there was some shaving cream left. *"Sådan!"* she exclaimed, with a satisfied smile on her lips, when she was done.

"Thank you, sweets."

"Are you going to shower now?" Lotte asked, observing Kenley as he grabbed hold of a towel and reached for a shampoo bottle from the opposite wall.

He beamed at her over his shoulder before he turned around and walked toward her. "Yeah. Want to join me?"

The color rose in her cheeks. "Your shower isn't really practical for wheelchair users. But your bathtub on the other hand ..." When Kenley was close enough she put her arms around his neck and ran her fingers through his hair. "I know you're more of a shower person, but ..."

"I guess I've never seen a reason to sit in a bathtub all alone," he mumbled as he inched forward and buried his face against her neck.

"Lucky for you I'm a lot of fun then!"

"Let me just steal a bath bomb ... I happen to know where they're stored." Kenley opened the cabinet under the sink and searched for a small basket with his hand. It had at least fifteen different bath bombs in it, all with various scents and colors. "Choose whatever you please," he said.

Lotte picked up a few that caught her eye and tried to guess what they smelled like through the plastic foil around them.

Luckily there were tiny labels on them: grapefruit, blueberry, mango, strawberry and so on. "Any preference?" she asked.

"Nah, I trust you to pick a good one."

"Mango it is."

They stayed in the bath for ages—even a long while after their fingers and toes were all wrinkly. Time flew by as they played with the bubbles, splashed water on each other, gave one another foam beards with mustaches and shared some lingering kisses. Laughter bounced from floor to ceiling for hours that night. Talking and being with each other was easy, almost too easy.

Later in the night, she put her hand on his chest, right where his heart was. Then she tilted her head closer to his and whispered, close to his lips, how she could feel their hearts beat as one.

The little things in life.

* * *

The next day, Kenley was sitting on the sofa in his apartment, waiting for his mom to come home. The clock had struck nine and he could imagine it was pitch black outside the window behind him, since there weren't many weeks left of the year, making the days become shorter and darker. In the background, the weather forecast was on TV, but the only things really reaching him were: chance of drizzle, cloudy weather.

His mind was occupied.

Kenley believed that a person like Lotte was someone you met once in a lifetime; it was a level of connection and comfort he'd never felt before. Despite not knowing her for long, he couldn't picture a future without her in it—especially not after getting to know all the layers that she had beneath. He feared the day his heart would stop beating; anything could happen at any time. But he did know that he wanted to spend each and every day with her in the meantime. At least in one way or another.

Kenley knew no one was perfect, but was convinced she was perfect for *him*. His growing feelings for her had him holding the ring in his hand that he'd never even passed to his late betrothed. He wouldn't propose to Lotte just yet, but the night before, when he could hear Lotte snoring, he tried it on her finger, to make sure it fit. And it did.

The ring wasn't much for the world to see. It was old and made of gold, but it did have a beautiful engraved pattern on it. The ring had been his grandma's. It was one of the few things Delilah brought with her when she left everything she knew at the age of fifteen. From the stories she'd told, it was a promise ring her dad had made himself, which he later gave to his girlfriend, who then became his wife—Delilah's and Fajah's mom.

In the beginning Kenley wanted to propose to Joanne with that same ring. But knowing that she wanted a big diamond she could show off, a fancy dress everyone would remember and a massive ceremony he definitely couldn't afford, he held back.

Everything was always about the damn money.

Joanne would never have put the small golden ring he held in his hand on her finger. Not a chance. Looking back, he wondered why he'd ever wanted to propose in the first place. Kenley and Joanne shared many good memories together, but all the fighting and the values they didn't share, always came in between.

Lost in his thoughts, Kenley hadn't heard the door creak as his mother finally came home after staying way too late at work. "Why are you up? It's late," she said, walking into the living room.

He quickly hid the ring in one of the side pockets of his sweatpants. "I'm waiting for you."

"Is Lotte here?"

"No, she's at her place tonight."

Delilah stood silent for a few seconds. "Has something happened?" For once she sounded a tiny bit worried.

"Everything is fine. But you and I need to talk."

Delilah walked back into the hallway and hung her jacket on the clothes rack and hoped, during the seconds she was gone, that her son would change his mind and maybe postpone whatever he wanted to talk about, until the next day. But walking back into the living room, she realized that wouldn't be the case.

"I know you're working overtime and trying to pay off the mess I've caused. Please stop doing that."

"I-I'm really tired, Kenny. Can we maybe talk about this tomorrow? I'm just ... I'm just so tired."

Kenley made a gesture with his hand, trying to show his mom he wanted her to sit down next to him. She always came up with excuses; he'd let it slide for too long.

Reluctantly Delilah sat down on the sofa next to him and said, "I just want to help you ... Your life is hard as it is ... please let me."

Kenley shook his head. "It's not worth it. I'm losing my mom in the process. You've been acting like a different person since the accident. I can't deal with it for much longer."

Delilah leaned back on the sofa and shielded herself by crossing her arms over her chest, hesitant to reply.

Kenley had built up more and more rage inside of him about the subject the more time that had passed, which made it hard for him to control his anger. His mom not having anything to say made him want to burst. "This behavior has to stop. Is it so hard to be at least a bit nice to Lotte?" He was breathing heavily, trying to find the right words in the mess going on in his head, but the burning feeling in his chest couldn't stop him from shouting, "You barely speak to her and when you do, you make her feel unwelcome! What is wrong with you?"

Delilah blinked back tears. "I'm sorry," she said, her voice shrill. Looking over at Kenley she could see he regretted raising his voice, from his clenched jaw as he bent his head down. "You have all the right to express your anger. I know I've failed at many things when it comes to being your mom." She wished she'd never isolated herself. She wished she had been there for him from the start. She wished she wasn't weak and an emotional wreck. "I want to do better. I'll try, for real this time."

Kenley forced a smile as he felt his mom place her hand over his. "You really like Lotte, huh?" she asked.

He pulled his hand away from her grip. "Everyone with eyes has seen that, except for you."

"I've seen it too," she stammered. "It's just hard to ... accept this change."

Joanne had been important to Delilah too; they were good friends. To her, it felt like Kenley picked the first replacement he could find. In her mind it was definitely not fair to Joanne. But seeing his face light up, week after week, whenever he talked about Lotte, or each time she entered the room, made Delilah understand that she was probably more than that.

Hundreds of "what-if's" had occupied Kenley's thoughts ever since the accident. What if he had been true to himself way earlier? Maybe the crash never would have happened? But if he hadn't been in that accident all those months ago, he would never have met Lotte, her family and their friends from the support group. Kenley had never thought that he one day would be okay with the fact that the crash had occurred. Was it wrong of him to feel that way? Sometimes he felt like a horrible person; he felt so guilty. But he wanted nothing more than to be happy. Done was done after all. He couldn't change the past, only his mindset for the future.

"Sorry if I'm changing the subject, Kenny, but ... your dad told me he was going to call you this week—"

"He hasn't called." Kenley shook his head in disbelief. "Why don't you dump him? We are his second choice. When are you going to realize that?"

"Don't talk about your father like that ..."

Kenley sighed loudly and covered his face with his hands before he snarled, "He's going to leave when you least expect it, like he always does. Stop defending him!"

Delilah stared into space and set her eyes on a picture on the wall in front of her, trying to think of anything else than her heart shattering, like a fragile glass slipping from her hands. Kenley not being able to see her facial expressions made it easier to keep the feelings intact, but as soon as she moved her lips, her voice trembled. Her delayed reaction said more than a thousand words to her son.

Growing up with an absent father had many times made Kenley feel like he wasn't good enough. He used to be gone for long periods of time, to later show up out of nowhere, just to stay for a short while. This made Kenley wonder why his dad didn't want to be with his family; he wondered if he'd done anything wrong. He still remembered how he'd once drawn his dad a picture of the two of them and how, later the same day, he found it in the trash can. A "normal" father would probably put it on the fridge, save it, or even frame it. At least that's what Kenley's old classmates' parents all did.

Kenley had told his mom to leave his dad several times. They had married twice, but after the second divorce they still kept on seeing each other. Delilah wanted their family to work, so she kept trying, in the hope of repairing what was broken. Kenley thought that his mom deserved more than someone who "loved" her for two months and left her behind for ten. In the beginning, he'd been worried, not knowing where his dad went. But after many years he couldn't care less about this man he barely knew.

Knowing he didn't prioritize seeing him when he was in town stung a bit. But he probably regretted many of his life's choices and didn't have the guts to meet up with his son; he knew what a horrible parent he'd been.

Kenley wished his dad would have been more involved, especially during his younger years, but he still felt incredibly lucky that he was raised by two strong women. He had his mom and Fajah, even though his relationship with Delilah was a bit strained from time to time.

Delilah put his arms around Kenley and gave him a bear hug from the side. "I'm glad you have Lotte in your life. I mean it."

Kenley hugged her back. A year earlier he found his mom almost annoying because of all the hugs she gave him each time they saw each other, but when she suddenly stopped after the accident, he started to miss those warm hugs a lot.

Delilah yawned and rubbed her eyes. "I think we both could use some sleep."

Kenley had tried the whole evening not to doze off on the sofa while he waited for his mom to come home. "You're right," he admitted, as he started to feel the fatigue he'd been trying to repress.

Delilah stood up and started to walk toward her bedroom, but she stopped halfway and turned around. She took in her son sitting on the sofa a few meters away before walking into her room and closing the door for the night, with a smile on her lips.

Left alone in the living room, Kenley took out the ring hidden in his pocket and felt the engraved pattern with his fingertips one more time.

CHAPTER SEVENTEEN

- ☑ As soon as he leaves, you miss him.
- ☑ You find his little quirks charming.
- ☑ You are more open to new ideas and activities.
- ☑ You can't get him out of your head.
- ☑ You feel comfortable and safe around him.
- ☑ You know you can count on him.
- ☑ You feel his pain.
- ☑ You are more affectionate.
- ☑ You plan for the future.
- ☑ You imagine whether your surnames are compatible.
- ☑ The thought of him makes you smile.

Result: you're head over heels in love with him!

* * *

Kenley sat behind Lotte on the edge of her bed and gently brushed her hair. He hadn't been in the same room as her for more than twenty-four hours, which was out of the ordinary; he'd longed for their time together the whole morning and afternoon.

"How was work?" he asked after a while.

"It was ... great."

"But?" He could hear in her voice that she was holding back, like she was debating in her mind whether she should tell him or not.

"I get this feeling that some people at work don't want to sit next to me during lunch and stuff ..." She tilted her head and looked down at her hands in her lap. Trying to sound more optimistic, she continued by saying, "Maybe I'm overreacting? And I mean, there is one really nice girl, she's an intern. She always sits down next to me at lunch."

It meant more to Lotte than the intern probably realized.

A few times others actually joined them, but it was after this girl had sat down, like they didn't want to be alone with Lotte, like she was boring—scary—or something. No one else took the initiative to sit down first, except for Fajah, those few occasions she had lunch at the same time.

Kenley stopped brushing her hair and set it over one of her shoulders, exposing the other one, since she wore an off-shoulder top. He hugged her from behind and placed soft kisses on her skin. "Don't mind those people. Seriously."

"Yeah ... I guess you're right."

Having his lips close to her ear, he whispered, "Or are you sure you don't have fangs?"

Lotte turned around, now being face to face with him. "I think you, of all people, would have felt them by now in that case." She gave him a kiss to prove her point.

His smile faded as he said, "Next time you sit alone, call me. I would gladly sit next to you ... or talk to you over the phone, so you feel less alone."

"Thank you, skat ... "

God, how he loved when she called him that.

"So ... how did the talk with your mom go?" she asked.
"She's the one picking me up tonight."
"I guess it went well then?"

That morning, Delilah had surprised him with bofrot for breakfast, made following her own mother's recipe; something she hadn't done in years. Delilah could only sit at the table with him for about twenty minutes before she had to head to work, but her actions showed him she was at least trying. The fact that she willingly sat down at the table to talk to Kenley gave him a sign that things were going in the right direction—the bofrot being just a bonus. It made him especially happy when his mom even volunteered to pick him up later that evening at Lotte's house.

He wanted to stay the night, since those nights when he slept next to her were the ones when he slept the best. But she had somewhere to be early the next morning, so he didn't want to be in the way. It wasn't just any appointment either. She was going to try out her new wheelchair—a wheelchair made just for her, hopefully a perfect fit. However, he did have a clever plan to think up a reason to stay a bit longer.

"Oh, before I forget! Fajah told me about this book she just read. It's a cheesy romance, you know, your type of book," he said.

"Oh yeah, that's definitely my type. I love fluff."

Kenley reached for his bag on the floor and fished after the book with his hand. "But the problem is that there's no audiobook. I just wondered if you might be interested in reading it to me?" he asked, as he handed the book over to her. Before he lost his vision, he used to read every night before he fell asleep. He missed reading, he missed following the words on the page, he missed being able to pick up a book whenever he felt like it.

"Why not?" she said, opening the book, turning pages until she found the prologue page.

They laid down in bed, under the enormous duvet, and snuggled up among the several pillows. It would be hard not to fall asleep for Kenley. Not because the book was boring, but because everything smelled like her, every word she read flowed smoothly and her body was warm compared to the temperature outside the window.

About ten pages into the book, Lotte read the sentence, *"If you love someone—tell them."*

She looked over at Kenley, but he'd already drifted asleep.

"What do you say about going to a party tonight?" Nova looked at her fellow group members with so much excitement, like she was a bottle of soda ready to explode at any second. "Oh, come on! Don't give me that look, you two!" She narrowed her eyes at Lotte and Kenley, who appeared very skeptical and would much rather have a night in—the introverts that they were. "Yes, you use a wheelchair, so what? And yes, you are blind. But that doesn't mean you can't party!" Nova shrugged her shoulders.

Apparently a friend of Nova was hosting this party and everyone who felt like going was welcome.

"The theme is the eighties, baby!" Ian added, as he grooved to imaginary music.

Lotte thought about what clothes she had in her wardrobe; at least ninety-five percent of the things she owned were black, gray or white. The thought of going to a party made her anxious, compared to her past self who would have dived in right away. The party spark had, for many reasons, died out. "I don't have anything to—"

Nova put her hand on Ian's shoulder and leaned closer to him. "Hush, hush, hush, can you hear all the excuses too, Ian?"

Ian smirked at Lotte and rubbed his palms together. "Leave

that to me. I swear I was a famous fashion icon or something in my previous life."

Nova snorted, but smiled when she turned away from him.

Seconds later Ian, with some help from Nova, began looking for inspiration on their phones, hoping to find a vibe which could fit Lotte.

Kenley gave her hand a squeeze, for her to know he would be there too. Him being by her side would probably make the party easier to endure. Then they could sit in a corner and talk, to make time pass by faster. There was no way she would "dance"; she imagined people would stare at her and wonder what the hell she was doing. It would be embarrassing.

Little did she know that her thoughts and plans were the opposite to what Kenley had in mind for the night.

Bernie sat in his chair and wrote down some notes from the group session, as he observed the conversation between the four group members from a few meters away. To him, it was clear Lotte and Kenley were a bit uncomfortable, but they could use the challenge—especially Lotte, who needed people to push her out of her comfort zone.

* * *

Later the same day, Nova went home to grab her make-up, a curling iron and accessories. At the same time, Lykke packed a bag full of clothes she knew Lotte wouldn't wear if she had the choice: colorful, sparkling things and T-shirts with crazy patterns and prints. Then Lykke rushed to catch a train, because playing dress-up with her short-tempered sister was something she didn't want to miss.

As they both arrived at Lotte's in the late afternoon, Nova spread all her stuff out over the kitchen table as Lykke hung all the clothes she had brought with her over the backs of the chairs.

Nova and Lykke had never met before, but they hit it off and worked well as a team—probably because they knew they had to work fast, so Lotte wouldn't have time to change her mind about going to the party.

Nova stood behind Lotte and made her best attempt to give Lotte some cute beach waves with the curling iron. "So, how's things with Kenley?" she asked teasingly.

Lykke stood in the kitchen and mixed some candy in a bowl for them. "Ooooo! Have you hooked up yet?" The kitchen being the center of the house most likely made her words echo through the whole place, especially since she almost said it louder on purpose, to provoke her sister.

Lotte shouted back, "Yeah, great, scream it a bit louder so everyone in the house hears!"

Nova, still fighting with Lotte's hair, trying to make it look decent, didn't like the sudden movements. "Ah, no no no your hair!"

Lykke walked back to the table with the candy bowl in her hand. "Sorry, but I can't help it. You're the only one with an interesting love life right now."

"Didn't you go on a date last week?" Lotte asked curiously.

"I don't know if she's my type. She's nice and all, but we didn't click." Lykke groaned and grabbed a caramel from the bowl.

"Who hooked up with who!?" Rasmus walked into the dining area, eating pasta from a lunch box. "Are you gossiping?"

Karla came running right after him and said, "Jesus Christ, Rasmus! Stop chewing with your mouth open!"

With his mouth full of pasta he replied, "We've been together for more than two and a half decades and you still have hope for me? Impressive ..." Then he let out a burp to annoy her—because why not?

Karla frantically looked for something in the kitchen, as she kept the conversation going by saying, "It's never too late to teach old dogs new tricks."

"Did you just call me old?" Rasmus scooped the last of the pasta into his mouth before he put down his lunch box on the counter with a bang. "I'm forty-five, Karla!"

Karla sighed and glared at her husband. "Says the man who freaked out because he found a gray hair in his hairbrush yesterday."

"Why are you grumpy today, skat?" He put his arm around Karla's waist and leaned in for a kiss.

She dodged his lips and gave him a kiss on the cheek instead, not to risk ruining her lipstick. "I'm late for a meeting." While putting up her hair with a hair clip she gave him a side-eye—but smiled on the inside. "I don't have time for this. Bye, weirdo. I love you." She ran to the hallway and hurried to put on her sneakers before she added, "I love you too girls! Oh, and nice to see you again Nova!" Then she rushed out through the door.

Lotte put her hands against her temples and stared down at the wooden table top, exhausted after witnessing just one part of the daily circus program at the Jensen's.

Nova needed to take a break from putting Lotte's hair up in a ponytail with a bandana. All of the laughter she was trying to hold in made her hands unsteady. Lykke continuing to tease Lotte about the "Kenley situation" didn't make it any easier.

* * *

The party was in an old, but newly renovated, barn with big windows which reached from the floor and almost up to the ceiling—making the sparkling disco ball and neon lights visible from the outside. The barn was built close to a small dock and since it was located on the other side of the lake that was flowing through the city, Lotte could see a few of the buildings she passed by almost every day reflecting in the water, with lights and a variety of colors blending together in the dark abyss.

Inside the barn, up-tempo eighties music was playing from several massive speakers and the soundwaves never once died throughout the night. There was a big, crowded dance floor in the middle that shimmered under the disco ball. People showed off their dance moves without shame, sang along even though they didn't know the lyrics, made out left and right—while others had clearly overestimated their ability when it came to consuming alcohol.

Nova grabbed a bottle of beer from the bar they passed by at the entry. "Come on! Live a little!" She took a sip and in a matter of seconds she, and her hot pink leg warmers, disappeared into the crowd.

Lotte wore boot cut jeans, a bright red printed T-shirt and a red and white bandana. She fit the dress code perfectly, but she was the only wheelchair user in the room. A few people glared at her as they walked by, like they wondered what her purpose for being there was; others almost tripped over her, since she wasn't at their level, which made her harder to spot in the dark and packed barn. Maybe she was overthinking, maybe those people actually weren't glaring at her, maybe she was overly sensitive, but it felt like a mistake being there.

* * *

Stumbling off the dance floor and walking toward the bar to grab something else to drink, Nova saw Lotte and Kenley sitting down at a table in the corner of the bar area. Maybe it was the alcohol making her more sentimental and dramatic, but watching the two of them being lovey-dovey made her wish she was sitting on her sofa at home, sipping wine from a bottle, listening to her *saddest of sad* playlist in the dark. Nova would do anything to one day be able to share her life with someone who would look at her the way Lotte looked at Kenley—someone whose face would light up when they saw her. Someone whose face would light up like Kenley's, when he heard Lotte's voice.

"If I were you, I would slow down with that …" Ian walked up to Nova at the bar and took her drink away from her.

Nova looked up at him with yearning puppy eyes. "It's a really good drink …"

Leaning against the bar with his back, staring at nothing special in the crowd in front of him, Ian said, "I get that, but last time we went out you ended up throwing up on me. I'm trying to prevent it from happening again. It wasn't the most charming thing in the world."

Defeated, she sat down on one of the bar stools. "I'm such a lightweight, I know," Nova snorted, before she faced the opposite direction in which Ian stood and examined the lovey-dovey couple over her shoulder again. "Not that it has anything to do with the subject, but it sucks being single …"

"I don't know about that … I feel kind of free to be honest."

She spun around on the bar stool and met the tall blonde's gaze. "Oh right, you're still single. How is that possible?"

"What is that supposed to mean?"

Someone must have turned up the volume even more inside the barn, because she had to shout to not be drowned out by the speakers. "You're hot, Ian … duh?"

"Did you just admit in public that you think I'm hot?" Ian shouted back.

Nova got up on her feet and stepped closer to him. "Your eyes shine through the dark … did you know that?" Surrounded by darkness, with only a few dim neon lights around them where they stood, she could still see those ice blue pearls so clearly. "And this area looks very kissable," she said, shifting her gaze to his lips.

He lifted her chin, forcing her to look him in the eyes as they spoke. "You deserve better, you know that right?"

Whatever had been going on between them behind closed doors, without anyone knowing, was hard to put a finger on, and lately it had become a bad habit for both of them. Nova swore the last time she felt his lips against hers, that night many weeks earlier, would be the end of it. But deep down she knew it probably wouldn't and she kept crawling back to something she knew couln't last in the long run; it was stupid, really stupid. She was wasting her time and his in the process. But hearing him talk about someone he'd been out with made her heart ache more than she thought it would—it made it hard to be a supportive friend.

It'd been too easy and was over so quickly, they barely had time to comprehend it all. They were opposites, but yet it felt so right. She wanted to be the one breathing him all in, but it was hard when he had his eyes on someone else. It should have been her.

"It's just a kiss, Ian." Nova cupped his cheeks. "And if you'd like … I can forget about it before sunrise. I'm used to that now," she said while faking a smile.

"Before midnight. Then you have yourself a deal," he replied.

"Deal."

Nova stood on her tiptoes to be able to reach him and he met her halfway. She never felt her body ache more than when she was starving for his touch. It was probably why it felt like the kiss lasted only a split second.

No one knew they'd ever been a thing, since they had agreed to stop seeing each other. In addition, whatever they shared hadn't lasted long either—so why was it so hard to let it go?

"Do you want some?" Nova asked, handing Ian the drink he'd taken away from her a few minutes earlier. "I know you don't drink much. But if you want to taste it …" she trailed off, beaming at him, doing a wobbly curtsy. "We've shared plenty of saliva anyway. Be my guest!"

Nova winked at him before she turned around. She spotted a clock on the wall. Then she disappeared into the crowd again. It was close to midnight—but he wouldn't leave her mind until way past.

* * *

The music wasn't as loud in the corner where they sat, yet Kenley had to shout for Lotte to hear what he wanted to say. "How many people are sitting here at the bar?" he asked.

Lotte knew the answer, but looked around them once again, hoping more people had joined them in the bar area. "Two in total." She could have lied, but Kenley would for sure have heard it in her voice if she had; he knew her too well.

"Come on then!" He stood up, unfolded his cane, and began walking toward the dance floor, where people had now paired up with one another, falling into each other's embrace, dancing to the slow tunes from the speakers.

"Where are you going?" Lotte shrieked after Kenley, as she saw him disappear between lights, fog and people. Her grip around the red pushrims of her new wheelchair tightened.

He heard her very well, but acted like he hadn't. He grinned, knowing she'd follow him—at least he hoped she would.

Lotte grabbed his hand so as not to lose him in the crowd, but in response he lifted it up in the air. She frowned, but played along, by spinning around with her wheelchair, doing a pirouette —like she did that night when they danced together in the kitchen. But this time it was different. They weren't alone.

Others could actually see her.

She wanted to be able to dance close to him. She wanted to be able to jump into his arms and kiss him like the couple next to them. She wanted to be able to feel his body against hers and not be separated by the distance she couldn't shorten. She wanted to do all the things she couldn't do.

Lotte's first thought was that she wanted to hide, but she'd been hiding for too long. So she gave in and matched Kenley's not so elegant dance moves, as they moved in sync with one another.

It was just them.

Her and him.

Him and her.

Toward the end of the song, Kenley scooped her up in his arms, and she put her arms around his neck. Him being tall made Lotte see above the crowd for once, but she couldn't keep her eyes off him. Kenley was dreamy and he made Lotte have mini heart-quakes whenever he was around. Everything with him was so much better than any fantasy; his touch was always so tender and his kisses so soft. Lotte thought she lived her life to the fullest before the crash, but she had never felt as alive as she did the night of that party, when she was in his arms.

She could see forever in his eyes.

"You know I love you, right?" she asked, hoping he wouldn't hesitate with his reply, as she let out the words that had been right on the tip of her tongue for a while.

Kenley answered in a heartbeat and in an attempt to charm her even more he, with a small pause between each word, said: *"Jeg elsker også dig."*

CHAPTER EIGHTEEN

Their new lifestyle was rather time consuming. Lotte worked and Kenley had started taking braille courses, slowly picking up the studying again. It made the late evenings—the few hours before they went to bed—the only time they had for one another.

Because of their busy schedules they couldn't see each other every night either, which was rather draining for people whose love languages were physical touch and quality time. So, after a few weeks, Kenley moved into Lotte's house, making it feel even more like home. Her house was big, there was more room than needed for the people already living under the roof anyway.

All the busy days made time slip through their fingers, and all of a sudden, the grass was greener, the days were longer, more sunny, and the tulips in the garden had begun to bloom.

All of a sudden, it was the first month of spring.

* * *

After each session they usually got picked up by Rasmus or Karla. But one evening, no one showed up. Lotte called her parents and when they finally picked up the phone, they told her they would be late, very late, for whatever reason.

The day Lotte and Kenley had first met, when she'd guided him through the city for the first time, onto the old bridge, she'd told him that they definitely had to visit the café at the other end of the bridge—her treat. But they hadn't done that yet, despite dating for nearly half a year. So, since they probably had to wait a while for someone to pick them up anyway, why not seize the moment?

Lotte smiled when he told her about the idea. Kenley stood up from the chair where he sat, unfolded his cane and then he walked outside the building with *"his eyes."*

"What does it look like?" Kenley asked, as he stopped walking to stand still on the wooden and steel bridge in the middle of the city.

Leaning against the bridge railing, she replied: "The sunbeams reflect in the water in such a brilliant way. The water almost looks light pink, with a touch of purple and orange. Like the sky right now. It looks peaceful."

Just like it did that day they first met.

Peaceful. Kenley didn't feel peaceful at all. His palms were sweaty, his muscles tense and he'd stuttered a lot the whole day. His mind was elsewhere.

First task: Do not drop the ring into the river. That would definitely suck.

Kenley turned toward Lotte and said, "Let's grow old and wrinkly together."

There were ten seconds of silence—yes he counted them all—before she answered, "Where's my ring then?"

To her surprise, and to his relief, he took out the small golden ring from the inside pocket of his jean jacket, got down on one knee, grabbed her hand in his and asked her to marry him.

CHAPTER NINETEEN

Her heart sped up at the fact that she wore a ring on her finger. She was silent for at least a minute, looking at it, trying to come up with the right words, watching it shimmer in the glow from the setting sun.

With an exaggerated, deep husky voice, Kenley jokingly said, "Perfect, now everyone will know you're mine." He chuckled as he put his hand over hers, moving it gently, to be able to feel the ring.

She grinned and tried to control the incoming giggle attack. "Who knew Kenley Kimathi could sound like such an alpha male?"

He turned to her from his place on the ground, shaking his head, and said, "Oh no, don't compare me to one of those wolf-human-mafia-billionaire-men you read about."

"You know I love all my fictional husbands, but I love you more. You're a million times better, skat." Leaning forward, she gave Kenley a kiss on his forehead.

He wished he could have seen Lotte's reaction when he proposed, seen her face light up and seen her admire the ring. But at least he could feel the heat coming from her flushed cheeks when he took her face in his hands and kissed her deeply, and could hear her heart racing inside her chest when they embraced.

That was more than enough.

After a little while, when Lotte had let it soak in that she actually was going to get married to the man she loved, tears welled up in her eyes. "Not many would do this ..."

Kenley turned to her. "Propose?" he asked.

"Want to marry someone they can't see." Lotte let the happy tears fall down on her cheeks. "Sounds like some reality program on TV."

The corner of Kenley's mouth curved into a smile. "Love is so much more than just being visually attracted to the other person."

She glanced down at her ring shimmering in the sunset light. "I ... I know. This ... It feels surreal."

"I love you, because you are you, sweets," he said.

"I love you more," she cooed back at him. She had to press her lips together not to shout it out, or end up hysterically laughing again, and accidentally scare the old man walking past them.

"But I love you the most. This is a fight you can't win," he told her, deep down knowing she wouldn't give up that easily.

They stayed at the bridge for a while and let the fresh and chilly evening breeze fill their lungs, before they left for the café on the other side. After treating themselves and celebrating with vanilla buns and chocolate cupcakes, Lotte and Kenley went to Delilah's apartment a few blocks away, as darkness began to spread over the city.

They took the elevator up the stairwell as usual, but as Kenley opened the door to his mom's apartment, not only two, but three people were standing in there. Delilah, Fajah and an unknown man Lotte didn't recognize.

The man had similar facial features as Kenley, but with a

shaved head, beard and no gap between the front teeth. Fajah didn't look pleased as she stood with her arms crossed, while Delilah twirled some of her hair around her finger, looking down at the empty kitchen counter.

The man stepped forward and with open arms he said, "I heard my son is getting married, eh?"

Kenley sighed loudly and his grip around the handles of Lotte's wheelchair tightened when he heard the familiar, yet unfamiliar, voice of his dad. "Why are you here?" he hissed.

"Oh come on! Don't start with that tone. I wanted to visit my son. I can't do that anymore, or what?"

"Bad timing." The look on Kenley's face said enough. If he could have chosen then to vanish into thin air, he would have. His lips were trembling as he said, "Sorry, I just … I just need a moment alone," before letting go of her wheelchair and walking past everyone in the apartment, to his room.

His dad looked over at Delilah and shrugged. "At least I tried?" He turned around, faced Lotte and mumbled some sort of half-hearted apology.

Fajah let out a disappointed sigh as all of them heard Kenley's door slam shut down the corridor. "Try harder," she said, completely done with the man in front of her.

Kenley's dad approached his son's room, to give it another shot. He knew that the next time he paid them a visit would be several months away. He knocked and Kenley let him in—because he knew it too.

Left in the hallway was Lotte. She bit her lip, somehow she could feel Kenley's pain. Talking about his dad was something he often tried to avoid, she knew their relationship wasn't the best and that his dad often showed up out of nowhere, to later leave without saying goodbye. She understood why he reacted the way he did; she couldn't even imagine how she'd feel if her own dad acted that way.

Lotte was lost in her own thoughts; she hadn't noticed Delilah walking up to her. "I want to apologize," she said.

"Oh uh, it's okay ... I-I know everything has been hard for you too," Lotte stuttered.

"Maybe we can start over? I would love to get to know you." Delilah made an attempt to form a smile on her lips. "I'm truly sorry for everything."

Lotte nodded, trying to mirror Delilah's expression, but it was easier said than done when her heart and mind were in another room at that moment. "It's fine. Sounds great."

Delilah dragged a chair from the kitchen table toward her and sat down in front of Lotte. "Oh, congratulations by the way," she said, pointing at the ring.

"Thank you ..."

"It came to mind that an old friend owns a bridal shop about an hour away. I can book a meeting with her if you'd like?" It was clear Delilah was afraid of saying the wrong things, after her many mishaps. She talked slowly, with a lowered voice and couldn't stop fiddling with her hair in one way or another. "If you want me to be involved, I can be there to help?"

"Of course, I would love it if you want to come along," Lotte said right away, without thinking twice—getting to know Kenley's mom was something she really wanted.

Fajah joined the conversation. "I'm inviting myself. I'm the one with the fashion sense in this family," she claimed, leaning against the wall next to her, smirking at Delilah.

Delilah looked up at her sister and gave her that type of glare Lotte recognized as the one she used to give her own sister when she said something she wasn't very fond of. But Delilah couldn't keep her tough guard up for long, she burst out laughing and said, "Is that your way of telling me I dress like an old lady?"

"You *are* old, Lala," Fajah teased, before she ran and hid

behind the small kitchen island as she heard Delilah mutter at her comment.

Watching as the sisters continued to playfully nag on each other made Lotte realize how thankful she was. How thankful she was that she'd repaired what was broken with her sister before it was too late. How thankful she was for her family who had taken care of her, when she couldn't take care of herself. How thankful she was for every other person who had helped her along the way to reach the point she was at now. And of course, how thankful she was for Kenley; he was the greatest gift she could've ever received.

As the three of them sat in the living room and waited for Kenley's bedroom door to open, Lotte daydreamed about what their future wedding could look like. She thought about the tiny details, but who were they really for? Her choice of dress wouldn't matter much either. Kenley would most likely never be able to fully see it all.

* * *

Lotte peeked into his room. Kenley sat on his bed and leaned against the headboard. In one hand he held his sketchbook and in the other a pencil—not an unusual sight. But he didn't appear as calm and relaxed as he usually did. From Lotte's angle it looked like the pencil strokes he made would easily leave traces on the other papers underneath.

"What are you drawing, skat?"

"Nothing special …" he said, putting the sketchbook to the side.

"Can I see?"

Kenley nodded and moved to the edge of the bed to help Lotte up. "I'm sorry about how the evening turned out, sweets."

"Nothing could ever take this amazing feeling away from

me." She rested her head against his shoulder as he embraced her. "How did your talk go?" she asked. Lotte mentally prepared herself for a not-so-good answer, since his dad had stormed out of the apartment ten minutes earlier without saying much.

Kenley took a deep breath and gathered his thoughts before he stated, "He just repeated his promises and lies." That was all his dad had ever done since Kenley was born.

Lotte ran her fingers through his curly hair and for a couple of minutes they sat like that, in silence, until she could feel his heart rate slowing down.

A moment later, Kenley reached for his sketchbook and gave it to her. They laid down on the bed and he nuzzled his face into the side of her neck as she flipped through it, looking at his drawings and sketches. Kenley had never shown the inside of his sketchbook to anyone before, so at first he felt a bit vulnerable and exposed. But hiding it forever from Lotte's curious character was an impossible task—and he finally wanted her to see.

With raised eyebrows Lotte observed all his illustrations. He may not have been able to fully see, but he still managed to create something much better than she would ever be able to. Sometimes the sun was pink, the water green, the trees blue and every now and then things were out of proportion, but it added charm to his drawings. The first pages in the sketchbook were dark, all drawn by the same gray pencil, but a few pages in, the illustrations became brighter—he must have used at least a dozen different colors. The sad girl on page two was forgotten already by page ten, where Kenley had drawn a bridge and a sunset, which he'd named *Ten Past Two*.

"There are still plenty of blank pages, do you want to add anything to the collection?" Kenley asked, reaching over his pencil case to Lotte.

"Oh believe me, drawing is not my strong suit!"

"You can always try? And, it's not like I mind having a

drawing by Lotte Jensen in my sketchbook. You know, I could probably sell it for a good price if I wanted to."

She let out a laugh and gave him a friendly shove on the arm.

After searching in the pencil case for the colors she wanted to use, she began to drag one of them carefully over the piece of paper in front of her. "If you got a chance to be able to see again ... would you take it?" she asked. The thought came to her mind as she tried to think of how she could explain whatever she was drawing to Kenley. She hoped it didn't come off as insensitive.

He was silent for a few seconds, like he had to think it through a few more times, weigh his words, before he answered. "I'm happy as it is. I don't need more than this. I have everything I need."

Talking to Kenley about a possible eye surgery was like shooting a ball against a wall and each time watching it bounce back. Lotte thought it was great he'd come to terms with his situation, but she couldn't help thinking about what would happen if he one day wanted to go through surgery, or if he one day got his sight back. It had been a while since his accident occurred, so yes, it was less likely things would go back to how it used to be.

But miracles did happen.

She was afraid she would become a burden—a problem. That she wouldn't be able to help him as much as he would have to help her. Afraid he would be disgusted by her scars. Afraid that he'd be disappointed with what she looked like ... if it didn't compare to what he'd imagined. He was the kindest soul she knew, but her insecurities were hard to overcome overnight. It would probably take a while.

Despite that, she truly wished for him to be able to see—if only once.

Kenley had fallen in love with Lotte through four out of five of his senses. He had heard her voice, smelled her scent, tasted her and touched her. But he had no clue what the woman he'd proposed to looked like.

Something that terrified Lotte even more, was if Kenley went through surgery and then lost the little light he *could* see. What if it only got worse?

Miracles did happen—but was it worth the risk?

CHAPTER TWENTY

On a balmy night in April, they stayed up later than usual one night, sitting curled up under a blanket out on the porch. They whispered vows they came up with right there and then to each other, with all the stars above as their witnesses.

In May Lotte found her dream dress. Off shoulder. Modern. With embroidery and a pattern Kenley could feel and follow with his fingertips.

In June they tied the knot officially, with their closest family and friends around them. When you know, you know—why bother waiting?

In July they adopted an older German shepherd without a home. Koda wasn't a service dog, but was very well behaved and could help both Lotte and Kenley with things in their day-to-day lives.

In August they bought their own beach house, but couldn't move in right away since the wheelchair accessibility renovations would take some time.

In September, after months of questioning himself about what Lotte had asked him months earlier, he'd come to the conclusion that it was worth the risk. He would do anything to be able to see her hazel eyes—at least once.

* * *

Five hours was an unbearably long time to wait for the result which determined if their life would take a major turn or not. Lotte sat in the waiting room, accompanied by Delilah, for the first two hours, until Lotte was finally invited to sit inside the room where Kenley laid in a bed, still anesthetized after the surgery.

For Lotte it felt like the hands in the clock hanging on the wall in his hospital room moved slower than usual. In the hope of killing time, she read a few magazines she found on the table next to her, listened to some music, scrolled through her social media feeds and fiddled with the ring on her finger continuously. She also made sure to send their loved ones updates in between.

It was starting to get late. Delilah went home to rest since she'd barely slept the night before. She was worried about the surgery, like any other mother would be. Fajah came to the hospital right after Delilah left and brought Lotte something to eat. But it was hard for her to swallow even tiny bites of the sandwich Fajah brought her. The more she ate, the more nauseous she felt. She knew that whatever the result of the surgery would be, it would for sure change their life together in one way or another.

Lotte wasn't the biggest fan of change. The thought of Kenley being able to see all of her was gut-wrenching, but mostly exciting, of course. She wanted him to be able to see her at least once, and preferably before she was old and gray.

* * *

Later that night, Lotte had read all of the magazines, finished listening to her favorite playlist, had liked all the posts in her feeds and even forced herself to eat the whole sandwich. Just as she prepared to shut her eyes for a brief moment, Kenley stretched his arms a bit and yawned, like he was waking up from an ordinary nap.

His eyes itched and filled with tears as he tried to open them, his head pounding at the faint light that came from the only lit lamp in the room, which was next to Lotte a couple of meters away. Almost right on cue, a nurse joined them and took some notes. The nurse explained to them that time would tell how successful the surgery had been. It could take days to see results, but sometimes the eyes adjusted quickly—it could vary from person to person.

The nurse gave Kenley a pair of glasses he could put on a bit later when he felt less dizzy. They weren't as cute as his ordinary ones, according to Lotte, but they would do a great job protecting what were now extra sensitive eyes. And that old pair of glasses might be history, anyway, if the surgery was successful.

When the nurse went out of the room to give them a moment alone, Lotte approached him slowly. "Did you sleep well?" she asked.

Kenley laid back down as the headache became worse. "How long was I out?" His voice quivered, as he was still a bit dozy.

"A few hours," she replied.

He faced her way, attempting once again to open his eyes. But they were so watery, that all the tears built up a blurry layer in front of what he could glimpse. "Have you been here the whole time?" he asked.

She caressed his cheek with her thumb and gave him a light kiss on his forehead. "I couldn't leave you, could I?"

Sitting next to the bed watching him fully waking up, Lotte's heartbeat became more rapid in anticipation. It could take days though, as the nurse said. But there was a chance he would recover quickly and be able to see her for the first time, without the usual blur, very soon.

After a while, Kenley tried to sit up, as his head didn't feel as heavy. He put on the glasses and blinked a few times, hoping to clear the tears and the blurriness. Much of it was still there and wouldn't disappear for a long while, but that incredibly foggy wall that had covered his sight for months, fell to the ground. It was like several new pixels had appeared since he last opened his eyes.

It would take weeks until his vision became more stable, but that night he saw those hazel eyes.

Clearer than ever before.

CHAPTER TWENTY-ONE

For ten seconds—yes she counted them all—they stared at each other in silence.

He didn't blink.

She didn't blink.

With wide eyes Kenley leaned closer and felt her face with his hand: first her jaw and her cheekbone, then her nose, her lips and finally the tiny scar on her right cheek. It was like he wanted to make sure it was really her.

"Can you ... Can you see me?" Lotte cried out. Her heart was bouncing so hard inside her chest that she could hear the thumps echoing in her head.

Kenley leaned back in surprise. "Girl, have you looked at yourself in the mirror?"

"Oh no, do I have something in between my teeth?" she asked, covering her mouth with her hand. "I just ate a sandwich ..."

Kenley shook his head. "You called yourself ugly?" His peripheral vision was blurry, but when her face was only inches away, he could see way more than just the contours of her: the edges of her face he had felt with his fingertips so many times, those lips he had felt the shape of with his own and those hazel eyes he had wished he would one day be able to see.

For a moment, time stood still.

They continued to stare at each other.

They froze, unable to move.

They tried to speak, but no words came out.

Kenley cleared his throat to break the silence. "I knew my wife was good looking," he said. "But no one warned me that my wife was smoking hot!?" His jaw dropped when he realized he wasn't dreaming, wasn't dead, but very much alive.

"This is so weird!" Lotte's emotions were all over the place. She burst out crying and laughing at the same time. It definitely felt like a dream. She waited for the moment when she would wake up and realize none of it had actually happened. "So," she began, after taking a few deep breaths, trying to keep her cool. "Do I look anything like you imagined?" She looked like she'd seen a ghost, with her eyes wide open, trying to read each small expression his face made.

"I-I don't know ..." The moment he saw her for the first time, he immediately forgot the picture he had created in his mind of her. It was forever replaced by the real version. "You're so ... You're so *beautiful.*" He reached his hand toward her face once more and let his fingertips run along her cheek and jaw. It was hard for him to find the right words as he looked at the woman in front of him. He was speechless.

Pure bliss combined with pure shock.

Lotte moved from her wheelchair to the bed so she could be closer to him.

Seeing her made Kenley feel like he was in seventh heaven. Tears were still streaming down Lotte's face and with somewhat good precision, he kissed them away. He tucked some hair that had fallen over her face behind her ear, lifted her chin and looked into her hazel eyes.

He could get lost in them any day.

Lotte leaned her forehead against his and let out that hearty laugh only he could make her do, as he whispered "beautiful" and all its synonyms right next to her ear.

Their want, and need, to talk for hours was cut short, as nurses came in from time to time, checking how things were going and encouraging Kenley to rest. He tried, but it wasn't as simple as that for someone who was afraid to close his eyes.

Later, when the last lamp was turned off and the dark and silence fell over the room completely, he tried to catch a glimpse of his wife. But it was too dim, and she was too far away, sleeping on a sofa on the other end of the room. He made an effort and tried several times to see something, even though he knew he shouldn't strain his eyes too much. But it was hard to tell whether what he saw was actually her figure, hidden under a blanket, or if it was his imagination deceiving him.

* * *

They stayed at the hospital until afternoon the following day. Fajah came and picked them up after Kenley's last check-up and drove them to Delilah's apartment, where they were going to stay the night. As they arrived, Lotte showed Kenley a few pictures from their wedding day, pictures of friends and family and their fur baby, Koda, who Lotte's parents had been looking after. It was surreal for Kenley to finally see the faces of the people he'd known his whole life again, to see those he'd met after the accident, and finally getting to see his own face after such a long time.

He burst into tears when Lotte showed him a picture of the two of them kissing, taken right after they got married, under the night sky surrounded by friends and family with sparklers in their hands. He didn't know if he should laugh with excitement or cry out of happiness—so he did both.

* * *

"Oh my God! I thought I had lost them!" After Kenley had looked through his wardrobe in his old room, he turned around and beamed at Lotte. He held a pair of what he called "fluffy socks" in his hand and he put them on his feet right away, almost tripping in the process. He wasn't used to the whole "having vision" thing yet.

As he laid down on the bed next to her, he realized she wore a sweatshirt and long sweatpants. It was still warm outside, even as summer had turned into fall, and she was quite a warm-blooded person; she had never slept in that much clothing before, not even during the previous winter. "Are you freezing?" he asked. Her facial expression and the fact that she had to think to come up with a reply, made Kenley understand there was another reason behind it.

"I just... I don't want you to get a shock seeing all my scars at once," she said, feeling the need to look anywhere but into his eyes.

She was mad at herself for continuously thinking about her body's flaws, especially since she knew in her heart Kenley would never judge her. She wanted him to see her scars. She just didn't know where to start.

As their eyes finally met he said, "Don't feel any pressure to show me, okay? Take all the time you need. I know this is a big change."

On the side of her stomach, she had a huge scar that continued across her back; a scar he'd already felt many times before. She pulled the sweatshirt over her head, leaving only a red cotton bralette to cover some skin on her upper body.

"First of all, I knew red was your color," he said, raising his eyebrows. "And secondly, how could you have missed this cool pattern right here?" Kenley moved his hand along her scar, but stopped halfway and put his finger gently on what now was a permanent mark on her skin. "That looks like a tiny galaxy!"

She looked questioningly at him. "A galaxy?"

"What would you say it looks like then?"

"A mess of forever-broken blood vessels and—" She trailed off, looking over at Kenley, seeing his less-than-pleased facial expression.

"Stop saying those things about yourself, okay?" He caressed her cheek and looked straight into her eyes; she didn't dare to blink. "You have to believe me now, beautiful. I can see you … which is still surreal." For the first time he could see her cheeks turn scarlet. It made his smile grow wider. "This close," he said, inching closer. "I can see you. *You*, you."

"Okay."

"Okay?"

She beamed at him, making those laugh lines visible, for him to see. "I believe you."

If someone could make her heart race, set her skin ablaze and make her veins pulsate, it was Kenley. The slow deep kisses they shared that night and the way he whispered sweet nothings in her ear, truly made her feel better about herself. It boosted her confidence more than she thought possible. The thought of covering the parts that were bare didn't cross her mind as he watched her with nothing but adoration.

Like the previous night, Kenley was afraid that once he closed his eyes, that dark and blurry vision would come back. So instead, he stayed awake, watching Lotte doze off beside him. He felt a bit creepy at first, not taking his eyes off her. But it was hard when she looked so adorable, cozied up under the duvet, looking like a butterfly in a cocoon.

Beautiful human, beautiful soul.

In case his vision worsened, he wanted to make the best out of the time he had. He could finally see her. He had to savor every moment—savor everything about her. From her long eyelashes, to the freckles on her back, her wavy hair, along with her imperfections that made her even more perfect—her scars. All those parts that made Lotte the woman she was. All those things he had never seen before.

"What time is it?" Lotte asked, sleepily. She woke up from her slumber as she felt Kenley move around next to her.

The lamp on his nightstand was still on.

Kenley looked over his shoulder to peek at the clock. "Oh eh ..."

"You watched me sleep, didn't you?" She poked him right in the belly button, just to tease him.

"I might have," he said, defeated.

"Don't worry, I've watched you sleep too. We're even." She beamed at him and he mirrored her. "But now ... you have to rest your eyes."

He hovered over her and put his elbows on each side of her. "What if I'm afraid to close them?"

"Hopefully, your vision will only improve from here," she said. "We need to take one day at a time."

He nodded and took her in once more. He had memorized her face well at this point. It was imprinted on his mind. "You're right. *Brick by brick.*"

"Maybe we can go through the instructions from your doctor one more time? I put the notes from her on the kitchen table. Could you go and get them please?" she asked.

Kenley rolled over to his side, threw his legs over the edge of the bed and stood up. He began walking toward the door, but stopped halfway and turned around.

Their eyes met. "What?" she asked, giggling.

"I just wish that one day, you'll be able to see yourself the way I do," he said.

Her lips were covered by the duvet, but he could tell she was smiling underneath by her eyes. "I hope so too," she said.

CHAPTER TWENTY-TWO

"Who are you texting?" Fajah put her elbows on the big wooden desk in her office, watching Lotte beam at her phone screen on the opposite side.

"It's Kenley."

"What does he want? Tell him your boss will get grumpy if you don't work."

"Will do," Lotte said. She looked down at her phone and smiled at the fact that Kenley used the same mix of emojis as her grandma did. He always sent at least five per message, most of the time no less than seven. But it was charming and she wasn't surprised; it was a typical Kenley-thing.

Kenley's ability to see had gone up and down the first weeks after the surgery. Though, the past couple of days his vision had been much more stable. His eyes weren't itching, they weren't tearing up as much, and he could see better each day that passed.

He'd tried his best not to be on his phone too much and not to watch TV, since his eyes were still sensitive. But after he finally decided to start using his phone again, Lotte began receiving tons of messages. It was new and she wasn't used to receiving texts from *him*. The months before, she'd mostly received voice messages—something she hoped he wouldn't stop sending her, since she loved hearing the sound of his voice.

Fajah tapped her fingernails against the desk to get Lotte's attention, when she realized her gaze was stuck on the phone again. "So, what's making you smile so much, if I may ask?" Lotte's wide eyes and arched eyebrows made Fajah quickly add: "Or wait, on second thought, don't tell me. I might not want to know!"

"Oh no, it's nothing like that!" Lotte reassured. "My parents are out of the house. He wants to make dinner so we can have a date at home."

Fajah pulled out her chair and stood up. "Oh! I'm definitely dressing you up for tonight then."

Lotte could feel her cheeks redden. "I don't think he's going to dress up, so I don't think—"

"Follow me," Fajah demanded as she began walking toward the door leading out to the main cafeteria area. "If he wants to show up to this date in sweatpants, that's his problem." She chuckled. "Not like he would care what you wear, I mean, your hubby would think you looked beautiful wearing a potato sack. I just think it will be fun and now I also have a reason for you to try on a dress."

"Are you sure it won't hold you up?"

Putting her hand on the door handle, she looked over her shoulder. "I'm a designer. If someone has spare dresses, it's me. Come on."

There was a whole room in the office with test samples of new and old clothing collections. There were several boxes stacked on the floor and placed on shelves, along with a number of mannequins; some of which were dressed like they were going to a fancy event, while some others wore loungewear. It didn't look organized at all, and nothing was labeled, but Fajah knew exactly where to find what she was looking for.

The dress Fajah handed over was a dark red V-neck wrap dress, tied together with a ribbon. To Lotte's surprise it hugged her curves perfectly. It was comfortable. It matched her lipstick. Looking at her own reflection in the mirror, the first thought that popped up in her mind was that she looked … *great* in it. A few of the scars on her legs were visible, but she couldn't care less at this point. They were a part of her and they added to the look.

Each one of her scars were a part of her story.

"How's it going?" Fajah asked from the other side of the draperies that separated them.

"I'm done. You can come in."

Lotte could hear the rasping sound of the drapery being moved to the side behind her and saw Fajah's jaw drop through the mirror.

She gasped loudly. "Girl … That dress was made for you." She walked in front of Lotte so she could take her all in, from all the angles. "Oh yes, you are wearing that, yes you are!"

"I actually … look pretty."

"Pretty? Drop dead gorgeous!" Fajah leaned closer and brought Lotte's hair to the front, letting it fall over her chest. "You always look beautiful, but I have to say … This dress … wow! I like how well it fits together with your jewelry and lipstick too."

"Thank you," Lotte said as her lips curved into a smile.

Fajah put her hands on her hips and smiled. "So, shall I drive you to your date ma'am?"

* * *

Koda was lying down on his favorite spot; the very cozy armchair close to the front door of the house. But as soon as he heard car sounds coming from the driveway, he sat up and looked out of the window next to him. Before Lotte could even grab the keys from her handbag, Koda was scratching on the door from the inside with his paws.

As Lotte opened the door, Koda looked at her with his puppy-eyes, hoping to be scratched behind the ears. "Easy, *søde!*" she told him, as she tried to get past him into the house. But Koda wasn't pleased with that answer and began rolling around on the floor instead, wanting belly rubs. Lotte had no other choice than to hunch and run her fingers through his fur. "Aw, have you not gotten enough love today, baby?"

Being busy playing with Koda, Lotte had missed Kenley approaching. He leaned against the doorframe leading into the living room and crossed his arms, ogling her from a few meters away. He was very much wearing a pair of sweatpants and a T-shirt, as expected. "Welcome home sweets," he said.

Despite the whimpers Koda let out when he wanted more cuddles, Lotte straightened her back and met Kenley's gaze. "Hi," she whispered. Noticing his eyes were still stuck on her she adjusted the dress a bit and fidgeted with the thin golden chain around her neck before glancing up at him again. "Fajah's idea." She giggled.

His pupils dilated, like he wanted to absorb all of her, every inch. "I don't mind," he said, raising his hands defensively in the air before closing the distance between them. "Dinner is ready, by the way. May I escort my beautiful wife, who might be an angel in disguise, to the table?" He leaned forward and grabbed her hand tenderly, lifting it to his lips and planting a kiss on the back of it.

Such a charmer, as usual.

She couldn't stop herself from beaming like a crazy person. "Lead the way."

Without hesitation, he scooped her up in his arms and carried her into the kitchen, bridal style. He put her down gently on one of the chairs around the dinner table, which he had decorated with lit candles, making it possible to see the plates under a mood-setting glow.

Kenley always made an effort during their date nights and he never left out *the little things*. That evening, he had lit one of Lotte's favorite scented candles and put it on the table, letting its aroma fill the room. He had also made her favorite dessert from scratch and added some decorations on top, to make it look "extra cute," like Lotte always said. It could be a pattern made with strewed icing sugar, a heart with a cream outline or anything with colorful sprinkles. Sometimes it took time to add that extra touch, but Lotte's excited squeal was enough reward and made it all so worth it.

After dinner they curled up on the sofa under a blanket, watched an animated movie and sipped on some non-alcoholic champagne in between, from their finest crystal glasses, just because they could. For a long moment, Kenley intertwined his fingers with hers and caressed a part of her hand with his thumb. But he stopped when he peeked over at Lotte and saw a frown forming, like she was deep in thought.

"Everything alright, sweets?" he asked.

From almost lying down and melting into him, she sat up and rubbed her eyes. "Oh, yes, everything is okay. I-I was … just thinking."

"What were you thinking about that made all those wrinkles appear on your forehead?"

"Does it sound weird if I say that I'm terrified of dying? I'm happy, I'm too happy. I'm so afraid something might happen and —" She was sitting still, but was out of breath. Her heart beat harder and faster inside her chest and she mumbled, not knowing how to continue the sentence she had started.

He cupped her cheek. "Don't you think it's a bit too early to think about death now?"

"It's just that I … almost faced it once and so did you. Things can change so fast." She bit her lower lip, trying to prevent herself from sobbing uncontrollably. "I don't like quick changes."

"You came into my life as lightning from above. Change doesn't always have to be bad."

"True." She blinked rapidly, hoping it would make the tears go away. "The thought still scares me."

He nodded and there was a moment of silence before he said: "It scares me too. But we shouldn't let it affect us this much. You know, a comet could hit my head and kill me tomorrow. We can't possibly be prepared for everything."

Kenley moved closer to Lotte and dragged the corners of her mouth upwards, forcing a smile on her face. She did that frown again, wondering what he was up to. "What?" she asked.

His lips parted, like he was about to say something, but he didn't. Instead he shook his head slightly and grinned at nothing special, before moving Lotte to his lap, legs on either side of him. He leaned back onto the sofa, put his hands on her waist and looked up at her. "We should just live."

"Just ... live?" She put her arms around his neck and inched forward. "You make it sound all easy peasy."

He shrugged his shoulders. "It can be, if you set your mind to it," he whispered, before closing the last bit of distance between them so he could kiss her on the lips.

How each kiss they shared could still make her mind feel all hazy, was something she couldn't put her finger on. He had that effect on her; his delicate kisses always left her completely spellbound. "Let's do that. Let's just live," she said, letting her body relax again, crisis averted.

He caressed her cheek and looked straight into her hazel eyes, which he could see clearly, even in the faint light from the lamp close by—they shimmered.

Since he'd gotten his vision back, he had barely done anything else but look at her, mesmerized by her beauty. But there was nothing else he would rather do; he would gladly love, cherish and admire her every day until he was no more.

After a little while he let his fingertips wander down her neck to her collarbone, which was bare since one of the sleeves of her dress had almost fallen down her shoulder. He embraced her, and pulled her even closer. During the remainder of the night, he continued moving his hands along the shape of her, and continued looking at her like she was the most precious thing he had ever laid his eyes on. At some point he loosened the ribbon, which was basically the only thing holding her dress together.

CHAPTER TWENTY-THREE

It had been several weeks since Kenley's vision returned. He'd decided to pick up his studying again, full-time, now that he could finally read all the material his professors wanted him to go through. But that also meant many mornings waking up alone, without him. Lotte didn't have to wake up as early as him each day of the week to be on time for work. At least she had Koda, who always saw his chance to sleep in their bed, next to his favorite human, when Kenley wasn't home.

As Lotte was about to take Koda out on his morning stroll, she noticed a small jar she had never seen before standing on her nightstand. On the glass of the jar, someone had written *"reasons to smile"* with a golden pencil, matching the jar's lid. There appeared to be many small, folded pieces of paper in it. She looked at the tiny tag hanging around the jar with a band and read it out loud: "Pick a note so you can have a reason to smile today, in case your stubborn self can't come up with any."

Of course he would do that.

The jar on its own was enough to make her smile. But she still decided to open the jar and picked a random scrap of paper and unfolded it. The message he'd written on the piece of paper, reminded her that she'd truly won the jackpot.

It's impossible not to smile when you think of me, right? Because I'm brightening up your life like the freaking star I am! =)

He sure did.
Kenley knew that with a simple smile, the brain released serotonin. It boosted the mood and provided plenty of health benefits; it reduced pain, stress, blood pressure and strengthened the immune system.

He knew there would be days when Lotte's sorrow would be out of his control, days when there'd be nothing he could do to make things better. He had failed at a lot in his life and given up on more things than he wanted to admit. But his mission, to make her smile, was something he would never give up on. He wanted to do everything in his power to prevent her heart from breaking if he could, which was the reason behind the reasons-to-smile jar. The same reason was behind the many times he'd put the empty toilet rolls he'd drawn hearts and silly smiley faces on around their room. He knew they made her smile; she found it odd and cute.

∗ ∗ ∗

Later that same day, after Kenley was done studying and Lotte was home from work, Ian picked them up outside their home and together they drove in the direction of Nova's stable. No one, not even Ian, knew why she wanted to meet up with them there.

As they arrived, they went to the paddock, which Nova had told them to do, in a text message she sent to Ian earlier. The surroundings were close to tranquil, the only sound being the singing wind, until the sound of clip-clopping hooves made them turn their heads. For years, Nova had walked next to her horse, not daring to sit on the back. But this day, she rode out of the stables, sitting in the saddle.

They tried their best to hush each other, to not accidentally scare the horse with their cheerful shrieks. Lotte's heart spun around and took a leap inside her chest as she saw Nova wave at them and almost twinkle from a few meters away.

As Nova came closer and gave them the green light, Ian approached her slowly. He brushed his fingers through the horse's mane before he looked up and locked eyes with Nova. "Want to grab coffee or something after this? To celebrate."

"Boy, you wish," she snorted and rolled her eyes at him playfully.

"Well that was passive aggressive," he muttered, as she turned down his proposal, looking very amused.

"What about Allison?" Nova asked.

"Just a fling," Ian replied.

She sighed loudly. "John then?"

He let out a chuckle, knowing what her reaction to this answer would be. "We broke up."

Nova shook her head like she'd officially lost all hope in him, and Ian continued his attempt to ask her out between the lines. Lotte and Kenley observed them from afar, both unsure as to what they were witnessing.

"Did you know they had something going on?" Lotte whispered.

"I don't know why, but I've always felt like they've had something more there, you know?" Kenley said, looking at Nova and Ian. "I can see that spark now."

Lotte looked up at Kenley. "Thank you for the cute jar by the way …"

"I wanted to do it much earlier, but it was hard when I

couldn't see anything. I didn't want to ask Fajah either, because—"

"Because you wrote some naughty stuff, or what?" she guessed, finishing his sentence.

Kenley laughed nervously and said, "Get your mind out of the gutter!" He began to walk toward the others, but turned around halfway and mouthed, "You're not wrong."

"Oh really?" she mouthed back, arching her eyebrows.

Since Nova was playing hard to get, Ian and Kenley decided to have a guys' night out instead. And, since Rasmus and Karla were away visiting some old friends, Lotte had the house to herself, for the first time in a while. She was accompanied by Koda, but he'd fallen asleep on the other end of the sofa.

While she was watching a reality show on TV, her phone suddenly vibrated as she received a new notification. She opened her email to check her inbox—and there it was. A picture taken about a week earlier. The picture of her that was going to be on the cover of one of the biggest fashion- and lifestyle-magazines. In the picture, she was sitting in her wheelchair, with her back turned against the camera; she was glancing a bit over her shoulder, showing off her side profile; she wore a top with an open back, revealing one of the biggest scars. She beamed at her phone in the dark, and began reading some excerpts from her exclusive interview.

Lotte Jensen Kimathi on her new life and finding love.

At this point she felt like things were finally starting to fall into place and that everything in her life was beginning to find its balance. She almost found it funny at first, how she truly believed her life was going in the right direction. It wasn't until she sat on the sofa that night and did a simple thing like reaching for the remote control to change channels, that she suddenly felt a sharp pain in her lower back. The pain radiated through her whole body, all from one single movement.

It was paralyzing.

She felt numb.

She couldn't move.

From sitting, she fell down onto the sofa, lying on her side. She tried to unlock her phone, but she couldn't with her trembling fingers. The cramps took over her body and black dots covered her sight. The pain was way worse than when a piece of metal had formed what now was the scar over her back.

The pain came from the inside. She couldn't stop it like it was a bleeding cut. It pulsated through every inch of her. She even felt a burning sensation in her legs—or maybe she just imagined it. She wasn't sure.

It was like her body wanted her to give up.

But how could she give up, when she had so much to live for?

Drops of sweat covered her forehead and her stifling screams filled the room. At the same time Koda woke up and started barking and howling—probably enough to wake up the neighbors.

After what felt like an eternity, she could hear keys rustle outside the door between the loud howls. She tried to open her eyes and part her lips to scream for help, but she had no energy left.

Her memories were vague, it all was a big blur. But she did remember someone yelling from a distance and someone shaking her shoulders in a hurry.

Déjà vu.

She could glimpse Kenley's face in front of her as the cramps began to ease, but she still breathed heavily with flared nostrils and could barely form words as her teeth were grinding. "Don't," she cried. She didn't dare to move. She couldn't move. "Don't touch ... It hurts."

Kenley's hands were still a bit cold after sitting outside at a restaurant and a bar the whole night. He put one of his palms on her forehead in the hope of cooling it down a bit. "Shhh, it's okay, sweets ... we're here now," he whispered.

Kenley ordered Ian to fetch something Lotte could eat and drink as soon as he saw her lying almost lifeless on the sofa. Ian was already at it, and ran around in the kitchen, next to the living room. The clattering sound of him looking for the things they needed in the many cabinets resounded through the whole house.

"This ... This is what you'll have to ... deal with," she sighed.

"Have you ever heard me complain?" Kenley asked. "Even when I'm old and gray and when my back hurts, I'll take care of you and scoop you up in my arms from time to time."

She still lay on her side, afraid to move. But she glanced up at him. "Do you know how dreamy you are?"

He chuckled, making those dimples visible, as he said, "Meh, I'm just loving my wife."

She beamed back at him in the dark.

CHAPTER TWENTY-FOUR

TWO YEARS LATER

Lotte and Kenley spent the day in Copenhagen, visiting Tivoli, the Little Mermaid statue, strolling around between the stores on Strøget and the restaurants in Nyhavn. They went to an ice cream parlor to grab some dessert before heading toward their red and white car parked on a side street not too far away to wait for their friends.

"You want some?" Lotte reached her waffle cone full of soft ice cream, topped with rainbow sprinkles, over to the driver's seat where Kenley sat, to let him taste it.

Leaning back in his seat again, he looked over at her. Those little moments always made his heart skip a beat. Like seeing her eyes light up when she finally got to devour the ice cream she had longed for the whole day and the smile that appeared on her lips since she thought the sprinkles made it look "extra cute." At times, it happened that she caught him looking a bit too long. His usual response was to shyly look away, pretending he wasn't—but it was obvious, and she liked it.

"Less grumpy now, sweets?" Kenley asked, knowing his wife just needed some sugar after a long day in the capital of Denmark.

"Hey, everyone can't be like you, sunshine!" Lotte grunted, but right afterwards she said, "Thank goodness for my grumpiness though, or else we wouldn't be here today." She gave him a satisfied smile before she continued her iced treat.

"Oh, you mean when you wanted a blind man to see you?" He chuckled and she answered with her, by now, well-known eye roll.

If someone had told Lotte three years earlier that she would be in Denmark, together with her husband and friends, with no worries to speak of—all before her twenty-seventh birthday—she wouldn't have believed them.

Of course, not everything over the past few years had been a bed of roses. They had their disagreements and bad days, but they were still head over heels for each other. They still hung out with the support group, they owned a beach house and a dog. Kenley could still see her with his own eyes, and they continued to make new memories together—good ones, that replaced the bad.

She couldn't walk and she would never be able to do so, but she had never felt more alive. Limited was something she was before the crash, she could now see.

At *ten past two* the worst experience of her life occurred—but it was at *ten past two* her life also began.

EPILOGUE

The sun had started to set and Lotte was on her way home after spending the afternoon outdoors in the company of a few friends. She wheeled her way toward the ramp that had been built for her many years earlier to make it easier for her to access the small beach house. The ramp was old and worn out, but it still worked perfectly for its purpose.

The sink in the kitchen and the one in the bathroom, together with the counters around the home, were lowered, to make it easier for Lotte to use. While in the bathroom, she grabbed her hairbrush, and as she brushed through her hair, she was surprised at how many gray pieces she'd received almost overnight; not to mention the wrinkles on her face not really helping her feel any younger, either.

On the other side of the door, there was an endless click-clacking sound of heels, walking back and forth around the house. A girl, with both personality and features from her dad, looked everywhere—or at least she thought—for the car keys. She wore an elegant, tight-fitting ruby red cocktail dress. Her long dark curls fell over one shoulder and she threw her handbag over the other. She looked at herself in the mirror, put on some

lipstick and spruced up her hair one last time. Not too much, not too little.
A mix between comfort and style.
"Mom, have you seen the car keys?" she yelled.
Lotte entered the living room and saw her daughter, Kendall, frantically searching through a drawer hoping to find what she was looking for.
Lotte knew exactly where they were. "Behind you," she replied calmly, as she pointed toward the coffee table.
"Oh, you're right! I thought I looked there already?" Kendall was the last one to use them, but she tended to put things in random places around the house, to later lose track of them.
"Be safe, okay?"
"I'm going to be fine. I'm staying the night at a friend's."
"What exactly are you going to do?" Lotte asked. She was referring to Kendall being all dressed up.
"This friend might have invited a few other friends too," Kendall admitted, almost embarrassed, hoping her mom didn't ask her any further questions and let her leave.
"Should I warn poor uncle Ian he might have to pick you up tomorrow?" Lotte laughed at the fact that her daughter was a spitting image of herself when she was her age. Lotte used to sneak out without her parents knowing sometimes though, so she was pleased Kendall was at least a little bit honest about her plans.
The thought of Kendall being in a car always made Lotte worry more than she should, but there was no need to. Kendall was a good driver and had always been, but her parents had, nevertheless, forced her to take several driving lessons—at least triple the amount her friends took. All to make sure she knew what she was doing and also to learn extra tips and tricks. Still, Lotte was scarred because of her own past experiences. Who could blame her?
"I won't drink." Kendall made an attempt to reassure her

uneasy mom. "That's a promise," she said, turning around and putting her hand on the door handle, making the Tabono tattoo she'd gotten on her eighteenth birthday—surprising her mother—fully visible from Lotte's angle; the tattoo Kendall and her dad had kept a secret for a while after she got it.

"I love you!" Lotte exclaimed. She had become a bit paranoid because of the tragedy that affected the family a year earlier. She always made sure to tell people around her how much she loved and appreciated them before they parted. Even though they would only be away from each other for a little while.

Kendall glanced over her shoulder back at her mom. "I love you more!"

She waved her daughter goodbye and said, "I love you the mo—" But before Lotte could finish the sentence, Kendall had already closed the door behind her.

After watching Kendall drive out of sight from the hallway window, Lotte made her way toward the bedroom—passing several framed photos on the way.

She always took her time and admired the memories that were right in front of her nose, yet so far away. She knew how easily life could take its turns and how easily the things she loved the most could be taken away from her, way too early. She'd learned to savor every moment, just in case she would never be able to relive it again.

Like that second summer after they moved into their house—when she'd rested her head on his chest, laying in the hammock that hung between the two blooming trees in their garden. She still remembered how Kenley had one foot in the almost too green grass, making the hammock sway from side to side, as a fresh sea breeze whistled by.

Or the winter about five years after that, when she'd sat on a bar stool next to the kitchen island, trying to focus on swirling saffron dough into buns, while she hummed something she'd heard on the radio that same day. Kenley managed, as always, to take all her focus away by holding her and kissing her favorite spots from behind.

She adored those little moments.

Lying down in the cold and empty bed had been the reason behind Lotte's many sleepless nights the past year. Each night, she wished she would wake up and realize it was nothing more than a nightmare and that he was still there, sleeping peacefully beside her. The pain she felt every night when she was the one who turned off *his* lamp, on *his* nightstand, couldn't even be compared to what she'd felt that day in May decades earlier. The crash had opened many wounds, but they all eventually stopped bleeding. But there was no way any of the scars he'd left behind in her heart would heal any time soon.

She missed when they both happened to wake up at the same time in the middle of the night, sharing whatever they dreamt of last, enjoying the feeling of being the only ones awake.

As the clock struck *ten past two*, Lotte had still not fallen asleep. She scooted closer to the edge of the bed and transferred to her wheelchair, before she headed toward the back door which led out to the porch. The sky was clear that night. She leaned with her arms against the fence, looked up at the stars and smiled, wondering if he was one of them, shining for her from above, as she listened to the sound of waves hitting the shore.

Kenley might not be there to see Lotte's eyes light up when she did something she loved for the rest of her life, but he'd succeeded in his mission: To make her realize it was possible to live a good life.

Racing excluded. Even after him.

ACKNOWLEDGMENTS

First of all, I want to thank everyone who has picked up this book, everyone who has supported my writing and everyone who has left nice messages about my interactive stories over the years. You, my friends, family and readers, mean a lot to me, and without you and your encouraging words, I wouldn't be where I am today. Because of you, I dared to take the next step and write my debut novel.

In the process of writing Lotte and Kenley's story, I've had a bunch of amazing women by my side, helping me with different things, to make it possible for me, and you, to hold Ten Past Two in our hands.

Mom, thank you for always believing in me and supporting my dreams, but also for sitting by my side during the many rounds of edits. I'm well aware I haven't been the easiest to deal with at times—your patience is out of this world. I love and appreciate you so much.

Beata, thank you for being one of my beta-readers and for starting my obsession with books. You're my hype-woman, always radiating sunshine. We are like fire and ice, yet you're the ketchup to my french fries. I don't say it enough, but I feel so lucky to have you in my life.

Lynn, thank you for taking the time to beta-read Ten Past Two despite your busy schedule, and for boosting my mood when I have been feeling down during this long book release process. You are, as you once said yourself, the Lilly to my Hannah Montana.

Lilia, thank you for always being there for me when I freak out—I'm pretty sure you're immune to all my spam at this point! You always know what to say and come with good advice. I'm so grateful for our friendship and I know I can always rely on you.

Elisabeth, thank you for taking your time to read Ten Past Two in its early stages, and giving me a lot of valuable feedback.

Britt, thank you for being the absolute best editor. I feel so lucky that I happened to stumble upon your page. I truly appreciate all the work you've put down, taking Ten Past Two to the next level and helping me, a lost non-native speaker, so much. You did an amazing job, and caught even the tiniest of details.

Daria, thank you for bringing my characters to life on the front cover. It has been over a year since I received the illustration and I still get starry-eyed when I look at it.

Dani, thank you for being so patient dealing with an indecisive mind like mine when designing the spine and back. They blend so well together with the front cover and I love all the colors.

I couldn't have done this without all of you. I appreciate you so much. You were the final pieces to the puzzle.

SHARE THE LOVE

Thank you for reading Ten Past Two. Please consider leaving a review, and if you enjoyed it, spread the word to a friend!

Instagram: @suelitawrites
Tiktok: @suelitawrites
Goodreads: Suelita Constance / Ten Past Two
Website: www.suelitawrites.com

Printed in Poland
by Amazon Fulfillment
Poland Sp. z o.o., Wrocław